"It was a long trip."

Dean heard a note of sorrow in Erin's voice, and wondered precisely what had caused it.

"You drove all the way up from San Francisco?" he asked.

She nodded, shooting him a quick glance.

"So what were you doing there?" As if he didn't know exactly what had kept her occupied all these years. Because somehow, in spite of all the girls between then and now, Erin had always hung, like a painting, in the back of his mind. Elusive and mysterious.

"Working as a graphic designer."

He wanted to ask her more and fill in the gaps between the last time he saw her and now. Wanted to know what had put those shadows under the eyes of the sweet, innocent girl who had turned him down with a sad smile. A girl who'd told him he had to turn his life around.

Well, he had. Just too late for her, he guessed.

Carolyne Aarsen and her husband, Richard, live on a small ranch in northern Alberta, where they have raised four children and numerous foster children and are still raising cattle. Carolyne crafts her stories in an office with a large west-facing window, through which she can watch the changing seasons while struggling to make her words obey. Visit her website at carolyneaarsen.com.

Books by Carolyne Aarsen

Love Inspired

Big Sky Cowboys

Wrangling the Cowboy's Heart
Trusting the Cowboy
The Cowboy's Christmas Baby

Lone Star Cowboy League

A Family for the Soldier

Refuge Ranch

Her Cowboy Hero
Reunited with the Cowboy
The Cowboy's Homecoming

Hearts of Hartley Creek

A Father's Promise
Unexpected Father
A Father in the Making

Visit the Author Profile page at Harlequin.com for more titles.

The Cowboy's Christmas Baby

Carolyne Aarsen

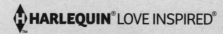

Recycling programs
for this product may
not exist in your area.

LOVE INSPIRED BOOKS

ISBN-13: 978-0-373-71989-1

The Cowboy's Christmas Baby

www.Harlequin.com

Printed in U.S.A.

In repentance and rest is your salvation.
In quietness and trust is your strength.
—*Isaiah* 30:15

To my sisters, Yolanda and Laverne.
Thanks for keeping me grounded.
And to my brother-in-law Jan, who bid on
the opportunity to be a part of this book.

Chapter One

It looked comfortably the same.

Erin McCauley parked her car in front of the Grill and Chill on the main street of the town of Saddlebank and turned off her car, her ears ringing in the sudden silence.

Though she had arranged to meet her sisters, Lauren and Jodie, at the ranch, she'd thought of stopping at the café to grab a soda because she was parched.

Her thirst was only part of her reason for her detour.

The other was that each mile she clocked northward from California to Montana increased the shame of the last ten months digging its unwelcome claws deeper with every roll of her car's tires. Now that she was so close she had to fight the urge to turn her car around and drive back south.

So she used the excuse of a pit stop to delay the inevitable surprise and questions.

I should have told them, she thought, her mind ticking back to a time when she was a more innocent girl walking down these very streets. *I should have told*

Lauren and Jodie everything that was happening in my life.

They would know soon enough, she reflected, stretching her hands out, making a face at her chipped nail polish. She eased her stiff and sore body out of the car and looked around the town with a sense of nostalgia.

The same brick buildings lined the street but the trees in front of them had grown taller and many of the flags flapping from their standards looked new. A bench and a couple of tables stood on a sidewalk in front of the Grill and Chill, but otherwise it was still the town of her early childhood.

A cool wind sifted down the street, tossing some stray papers and tugging a few leaves off the trees. It was mid-September. The kids were back in school and soon the leaves would be changing color.

I'm almost home.

The words settled into a soul in need of the solidity of this place. A soul disillusioned by life and by people. A soul that had grown tougher the past year.

The door of the Grill and Chill opened and a tall, lean figure stepped out, dropped a cowboy hat on his head and painstakingly worked his way down the three steps leading to the sidewalk. He moved with a pronounced limp, though he didn't look that old. His plaid shirt was sprinkled with sawdust. A leather belt and a large rodeo competition buckle cinched frayed, faded blue jeans that ended on scuffed cowboy boots with worn-down heels.

He was the real deal, Erin thought, mentally comparing him to the fake cowboys she'd seen advertised on billboards on her drive up here from San Francisco.

When he lifted his head sea-green eyes met hers and her world spun backward.

The face looking back at her was hardened by time, grown leaner over the years. Stubble shaded a strong jaw and his eyes were fanned by wrinkles from spending time outside. But Dean Moore still held that air of heedlessness. The tilt of his head, the angle of his battered cowboy hat showed her he still looked at the world like it was his for the taking.

Then he smiled, his eyes lit up and his features were transformed.

The old curl of attraction that she had always fought when she was around him gripped her heart. Her mouth, if it was possible, became even drier.

He walked toward her, his smile growing. "Hey, there. What are you doing here?"

Erin stared at him, surprised at his casual question. But to her consternation, even after all these years and all that had happened to her, he could still lift her heart rate. "I'm headed home," she managed.

"Vic said you were too busy to come to town. I thought you were getting ready for a visit from your uptight sister, if you'll pardon the little joke."

And then realization dawned.

He thought she was Lauren. Her twin sister. And she knew the exact moment he realized this himself.

His mouth shifted, his eyes narrowed and he visibly withdrew.

Crazy that this bothered her. Dean was so far in the past he may as well have been a character in the fairy stories she had once loved reading and drawing pictures of.

"My apologies. I thought you were—"

"Lauren," she finished for him. "Sorry. I'm Erin. The uptight sister."

He frowned as he assimilated this information, his hands slipping into the back pocket of his worn blue jeans. "Jodie and Lauren said you were coming this evening." He didn't even have the grace to look ashamed of himself.

"I'm early. Heavy foot."

He was silent a beat, as if still absorbing the reality of her presence. "So. How've you been?"

She wanted to make some glib remark about what he'd said about her character but didn't have the energy so she simply went with "Fine. I'm fine."

"Right." He gave her a tight smile, visibly retreating.

She shouldn't be too surprised at his reaction or what he'd said about her. Every time he'd asked her out the summers she spent on her father's ranch, she'd turned him down. He was a rough-living young man who rode hard, drank hard and played hard.

And yet, there had always been something about him that appealed. Some measure of self-confidence and brash self-awareness she knew she lacked.

In spite of the attraction she'd felt, her practical self had told her that Dean Moore was not the kind of man a good Christian girl wanted in her life.

And now?

She was hardly the sweet, innocent girl who'd left Saddlebank all those years back. Hardly walking with her Lord like she used to. She'd turned away from God nine months ago. When she'd found out she would be a single mother.

"So, you headed to the ranch?" Dean asked.

"Eventually. I thought I'd make a quick stop at the

Grill and Chill." Her mouth was even drier than before. Some soda or tea and a few moments to settle
her nerves before seeing her sisters was just what she
needed.

"Okay. Well, I'll see you around."

She held his gaze a beat longer, surprised at the
twinge of attraction he still created. The usual battle
of her head and heart, she thought. Drawn to the wrong
kind of person.

Then a muffled cry from the car pulled her attention away from him and to her baby still tucked in her
carrier in the backseat.

Erin opened the door and took a second to inhale
the sweet scent of baby powder and Caitlin's shampoo. With a gentle finger she stroked her baby's tender
cheek, still amazed at the rush of love this tiny infant
could pull from her. Six weeks ago she'd come into
Erin's life and since then regardless of the exhaustion
and confusion that dragged at her every day, Caitlin
had been a bright spot in a life that had, of late, had
some dark and hard valleys.

Erin grabbed the muslin blanket from beside her
and laid it over top so her baby wouldn't be exposed
to the wind or the sun, then gently pulled the seat free,
tucking her arm under the handle and straightening.

Dean still stood there, frowning as if still trying
to absorb the reality of her situation. His puzzlement
grew as he glanced from the car seat hanging on her
arm to her ringless left hand.

Yes, I am a single mother, she wanted to say, *and no,
this was not in my long-term plan when I left here that
summer. After turning you down yet again.*

Their gazes locked for a few heartbeats more as if acknowledging a shared past.

As she closed the door of the car he touched the brim of his hat in a surprisingly courtly gesture, then turned and left, his steps uneven, his one leg hitching with every movement.

She guessed this was from his rodeo accident almost a year back. Lauren had alluded to it in the texts they had exchanged the past few months.

Sadness winged through her. How much had changed for both of them since that summer, all those years ago.

She took a few steps almost getting bowled over by a young woman.

"Hey, Dean, wait up," the woman called and while Erin watched she ran up to him, tucking her arm in his. She was slender, tall, her brown hair shining in the sunlight, her trim figure enhanced by a snug tank top and denim pants. "You coming to the dance on Friday night? I was hoping you'd save a waltz for me." She slid a red-painted fingernail down his arm. Her head tipped to one side as she obviously flirted with him.

Erin recognized Kelly Sands, a girl a few years younger than both of them, daughter of a local, wealthy rancher. She remembered Kelly as a somewhat spoiled girl who loved a good time more than she loved the consequences of it.

"I doubt I'll be going to any dance," Erin heard Dean say, his voice gruff.

"Oh, c'mon. It will be fun. We can hang out. Like old times."

Then for some reason Dean glanced back at her and Erin saw herself through his eyes.

Hair pulled up in a sloppy bun. T-shirt with a ketchup stain from when she held Caitlin while trying to wolf down a hot dog. Yoga pants worn for comfort and ease of movement and flip-flops for the same reason.

Yeah. Not so much to compare to.

Then just as Erin was about to step into the café Kelly turned to see where Dean was looking. She frowned her puzzlement and then suddenly her smile grew brighter. "Hey, Erin. Wow. I haven't seen you in ages."

"It's been a few years," Erin admitted, her pride stung that while Kelly, who barely knew her, could see the difference between her and Lauren and Dean couldn't.

"And look at you. With a baby." Kelly let go of Dean's arm and scurried over, lifting the cloth covering the car seat. "Oh, my goodness. She's adorable." Kelly looked up at her. "I'm guessing from the pink sleeper she's a girl."

"Yes. She is."

"I didn't know you were married," Kelly continued, covering Caitlin again and, as Dean had, looking at her left hand.

Erin didn't want to blush or feel a recurrence of the shame that she struggled to deal with.

So she looked Kelly straight in the eye. "I'm not."

The girl released a surprised laugh, as if she didn't believe her. "Really? You of all people?"

Erin wasn't going to dignify that with a response so she simply kept her chin up, figuratively and literally, and held Kelly's gaze, saying nothing.

"I guess people really do change," Kelly said. Then

with a dismissive shrug of her shoulder she walked back to Dean. "And I'll see you on Saturday," she told him, her hand lingering on his arm.

Erin pulled her gaze away, wondering why she cared who Dean hung out with. But as she looked over at the door of the Grill and Chill, Dean's reaction lingered, as did Kelly's comment.

If she went inside she would probably meet someone she knew. And face more of what she'd just dealt with.

She couldn't handle more censure, puzzled glances and assumptions.

So in spite of the thirst parching her throat, she put Caitlin back in the car.

Then she headed home.

"Just drop me off at home," Dean said as Vic turned off Main Street, heading toward the highway and the Rocking M. "I don't feel like coming with you to Lauren's place."

"Home is twenty miles out of the way." Vic shot his brother a questioning glance. "And I promised Lauren I'd get these groceries to her as soon as possible. I guess Erin is supposed to be arriving late this afternoon."

Actually, she would be there sooner.

But Dean wasn't going to mention that to Vic. He was still absorbing the shock seeing Erin had given him. He still didn't know how he had mistaken her for Lauren.

Though they were twins, Lauren's eyes were gray; Erin's a soft blue. Lauren's hair was blonder, Erin's held a tinge of copper. And Erin had always had a quiet aloofness that he'd viewed as a constant challenge.

Seeing her again so easily erased the years since

they were last together. One look into those blue eyes and once again he was the brash young man who was willing to take another chance at rejection from Erin McCauley. Once again he felt the sting of her steady refusals.

And then she'd pulled the car seat out of the back of the car and he felt as if his world had spun in another direction.

He hadn't known she had a baby. Or that she was married, though she wasn't wearing a ring. Neither Lauren nor Jodie mentioned a husband.

When he'd taken a closer look at her, he'd seen the hollowness of her cheeks, a dullness to her eyes. When she'd told Kelly she wasn't married his world took another tumble.

Erin McCauley was always the unobtainable. Elusive. He had always known she was too good for him. And now, here she was. A single mother.

"I want to get working on that toolshed I promised Mom I'd finish," he said, wishing he could forget about Erin, frustrated at the effect she had on him. "And I'm tired."

He hoped his brother would accept his excuse and drive out of his way to bring Dean home but he doubted it. Vic was still in that glazed-eye stage of romance and would take advantage of any chance to see his fiancée.

"Tired and sullen from the sounds of things," Vic said with a laugh. "I'm sure Mom won't care if you're a day late on the shed. Besides, you didn't have to come to town with me today. I wouldn't have minded if you checked the cows in the higher pasture."

"They were okay when you rode up there last week. I doubt much has changed."

"We've always checked them regularly," Vic said but Dean ignored the comment. He had accepted Vic's invitation to go to town precisely because he felt grumpy and guilty about not checking the cows. But he had hoped Vic wouldn't nag him about not riding.

Dean hadn't been on a horse since that bad toss off a saddle bronc that had shattered his leg and put his dreams of a rodeo career on hold. Vic had been at him to continue his therapy, to cowboy up and get back on the horse.

But Dean wasn't about to admit to his brother why he didn't do either.

"I know we do, but I was busy. That's why I want to get working on that shed for Mom." He knew he was wasting his argument but couldn't give up without one last push. He really didn't want to see Erin again. Especially not after he'd made that stupid joke about Lauren's "uptight" sister.

"Then the shed is two days late instead of one." Vic shrugged, turning onto the highway heading toward the Circle M ranch where Lauren and Jodie were waiting for their sister.

If they did a quick drop-off he and Vic could be on their way home before Erin arrived. When he'd met her it looked as if she was headed into the Grill and Chill so there was a possibility.

But Vic was whistling some vague country song, which meant his brother was happy about seeing his fiancée again. Which meant Dean would have to watch Lauren and Vic give each other those stupid, secret smiles. And the occasional kiss.

He was happy for his brother. Truly.

But ever since his girlfriend Tiffany broke up with

him, less than twenty minutes before the ride he'd injured himself on, Dean had struggled with a combination of anger and betrayal.

Being dumped just before a ride that could have put him on the road to a major title was bad enough. Finding out that she was leaving him for his brother, whom she'd had a secret crush on the whole time they were dating only added insult to the actual injury he'd been dealt.

The fact that Vic and Tiffany hadn't gotten together after the accident helped, but knowing his girlfriend preferred his brother over him still stung.

And now Erin was in back town. Erin who seemed to prefer anyone to him.

Every summer since their parents' divorce, Erin had come from Knoxville to Saddlebank to stay with her father. And every summer, from the time they were both fifteen, he'd asked her out. And every time she'd turned him down. Thankfully his ego was more intact then. He kept thinking that his dogged persistence would do the trick, but when she told him the last time he asked her that she didn't approve of his lifestyle and didn't approve of him, he got the message.

He knew sweet Erin McCauley was above his paygrade and that she frowned upon his ever-increasing rowdiness, but at that time in his life obstacles had just seemed like challenges he could overcome. And Erin, with her gentle smile and kind nature, was exactly that kind of challenge. One that he'd lost.

He'd had girlfriends since then but deep down he always compared them to her.

His gold standard.

And now?

Pain twinged through his leg and he shifted it, grimacing as he did. Now he had even less to offer her or any other woman. A crippled ex-bronc rider trying to figure out what he was going to do with his life.

"So what does Jan have you working on these days?" Vic asked, pulling him from the melancholy memories.

"We're finishing up a hay shed for the Bannisters and there's a big job coming up in Mercy I'm hoping to get in on."

"You still enjoy the work?"

"It's work," Dean said carefully knowing that his brother was fishing. Again. Feeling him out about coming in as a partner on the ranch. That had always been the plan when Vic made a deal with Keith McCauley to lease his ranch. Then came the accident that changed so much for Dean. Now he wasn't sure what he wanted anymore or where he fit. Rodeo was off the table and he didn't know how much of an asset he could be to Vic.

If he couldn't ride a horse.

"Once Erin comes back Lauren and Jodie can make a final decision about the Circle M. And I was hoping you would make one, too," Vic returned.

"I thought their dad said in his will that only two of them had to stay two months." When Keith McCauley died his will stipulated that two of the girls had to stay two months on the ranch in order for all three to inherit.

"Lauren and Jodie both fulfilled the conditions of their dad's will, that's true, but I think they just want to talk it over with Erin. Out of courtesy." Vic waited a beat, then shot him a glance. "And once that's done, we need to make a decision about you coming in with me as a partner."

"I know. I need some time." Dean shifted in his seat

again, stifling his frustration as he watched the fields flowing past.

"You've had time. This was the plan," Vic continued, his voice holding an edge of anger. "We talked about it before I approached Keith McCauley to lease the ranch from him, and now that it's pretty much a go I want to expand the herd. But I can't do that if I can't get a commitment from you."

Dean knew he was stalling and understood his brother's exasperation. Ranching together had been their plan for the past ten years. When he'd dated Tiffany he'd imagined his life with her in the little house on one corner of the Circle M Ranch, tucked up against the river.

He had been working for Jan Peter for a couple of years as a carpenter and had already planned the renos he was going to do on the house after he and Tiffany got married.

But those dreams had been busted in two decisive moments. When Tiffany broke up with him and when he smashed his leg half an hour later.

"Lauren and I are getting married soon," Vic continued. "I need to know where we're at. If I need to bring in another partner or if you're still part of this."

"I know and I appreciate that you've been willing to wait," Dean said, staring ahead at the road flowing past rolling fields toward the mountains cradling the valley. "But I'm not sure where I belong anymore."

"What do you mean? You belong here. You're a rancher. It's your legacy and it's in your blood."

Dean released a humorless laugh. "And what kind of rancher can't ride a horse?"

Vic looked back at the road, his one hand tapping

his thigh as if restraining his impatience. "You just need to try again."

Dean's mind ticked back to the last time he tried to get on a horse. Vic had come upon him trying to mount up. He wanted to help and they'd had a fight. Dean had wanted to try on his own and his brother didn't think he could. Trouble was, Vic was right. And though he had come across all tough and independent, truth was he was scared spitless and secretly thankful for the chance to walk away.

"And lots of ranchers don't ride horses," Vic continued. "They use their trucks or quads—"

"You can't take a quad up into the high pasture or the back country. We both know that," he said, his voice hard. "Ranchers in this country ride horses. Simple as that."

And Vic's silence told Dean that his brother knew he was right.

"You'll ride again" was all Vic said.

Dean wished he had his sibling's optimism. Because right about now, he felt as if both Vic and his boss, Jan, were merely helping him out. Giving the poor cripple a hand up.

He wasn't used to that. He was used to being independent and doing things on his own. Like he had up until the accident.

And now they were going to see his brother's fiancée and the girl he'd once cared for. And he was coming as half a man.

Chapter Two

This was it.

Erin slowed as she headed down the driveway and made the final turn. She saw the house situated on the hill, overlooking the fields and the mountains beyond, and felt the land wrap itself around her heart and stake its claim.

She wanted to stop and take it in.

But Caitlin had been fussing ever since her aborted stop in Saddlebank and Erin never had gotten that drink.

She headed toward the house, parking beside a couple of smaller cars. She didn't recognize one but guessed it was Jodie's from the stickers on the windows and the beads hanging from the rearview mirror. The other one she knew to be Lauren's. Plus, in spite of the dust on the road, it gleamed in the afternoon sun. Lauren always liked things orderly and tidy.

Caitlin was screaming by the time she shut the engine off. Erin jumped out, quickly unclipping her car seat, grabbing the diaper bag.

The door of the house burst open as she headed up

the walk and Jodie and Lauren spilled out, arms wide, calling out her name.

And then stopped dead in their tracks staring at the car seat she lugged up the walk, Caitlin now howling her protest from within.

"Hey, guys. Can you take her? I'm parched." Erin unceremoniously thrust the car seat toward Lauren, gave Jodie a quick smile and rushed into the house, not even bothering to look behind her. She knew she was being a coward but she really was dying of thirst.

And she needed a moment.

She ran to the bathroom, turned the tap on and gulped down a glass of water. Then another. As she lowered the cup she caught her reflection in the mirror. Hollow cheeks, sallow complexion and hair that looked like she had been attacked by an angry squirrel. Of course Dean would have to see her like that.

And why do you care?

She cared because even though Dean was eminently unsuitable and definitely not her type, he'd always held an undeniable appeal. He represented a part of her that sometimes yearned to be cool. Accepted. Independent.

Well, you're not, she told herself, finger-combing her hair and with quick, practiced movements, tying it up in a loose topknot.

Sam liked it when she wore it down. And since she'd broken up with him, she'd deliberately started wearing it up.

Besides, that way Caitlin couldn't grab it.

A faint wail resounded from the living room and then the sound of her sisters hushing her baby.

She held the edges of the counter, dizziness washing over her. She blamed it on a combination of not eating for the past twelve hours and the nerves holding her in a steady grip all the way home.

She splashed some water on her heated cheeks, patted them dry, sucked in a long breath and left to face her sisters.

As she walked around the corner she felt a sense of coming home. To her left was her father's office, to her right the kitchen where she and her sisters had spent a lot of time cooking and baking and trying out recipes. Things they were never allowed to do at their grandmother's house back in Knoxville where they lived ten months of the year.

The living room lay ahead with its soaring ceilings and large windows that let in so much light. The huge stone fireplace dominated the one wall but no fire burned in it now.

Jodie sat on the loveseat cradling Caitlin in her outstretched arms. Lauren sat beside her, Caitlin's tiny fingers clutching hers.

"You are just the sweetest little thing," Jodie continued, bending over to nuzzle her cheeks.

Erin's heart softened at the sight of her sisters so obviously in love with her baby.

And the one thought threading through her mind was, *We're not alone anymore.*

Lauren sensed her presence and looked behind her, her smile stiffening as Erin came nearer. But then she stood and walked around the couch, her arms open wide.

Erin stepped directly into her twin sister's embrace, fighting down the surprising and unwelcome tears as Lauren hugged her. Hard. Tight.

"Oh, sweetie. What has been happening in your life?" Lauren murmured.

Erin simply clung to her sister unable to find the words.

She was the first to pull away scrubbing at her cheeks, thankful that she hadn't bothered to put on any makeup.

"Sorry. I just…" She looked at her sister and gave her a watery smile. "I missed you."

Lauren cupped her face in her hands and brushed a gentle kiss over her forehead. "Missed you, too, Rinny."

The pet name was almost her undoing again.

But then Jodie stood, shifting Caitlin in her arms, grabbing Erin in a one-armed hug. "Hey, sis," she said, pressing her cheek against hers. "Love this little girl."

Erin pulled in a shaky breath and struggled to keep her composure. All the way up here she'd been nervous and afraid of what she would see in her sisters' eyes. But now that she had arrived and her sisters had met Caitlin, she felt a loosening of the tension gripping her the past few months.

"I love her, too," she whispered, stroking her daughter's cheek.

They were all quiet for the space of a few heartbeats, each connected by this precious baby.

"So…" Lauren let the word drag out and Erin knew the moment of reckoning had arrived.

Then a door slammed and a male voice boomed into the quiet, "Grocery delivery," and Erin felt a temporary reprieve.

She turned to see Vic walking into the room, half a dozen plastic bags slung from his hands. He was as tall as Dean, his hair lighter with a bit of curl, his features softer and a brightness to his eyes that Dean didn't have.

He dropped the bags on the counter, then looked over the girls. He did a double take as he saw Erin, then released a huge grin.

"So you finally made it," Vic said, walking over to her. "Your coming was all Lauren and Jodie have been talking about the past week."

Then Vic surprised her by pulling Erin close in a quick embrace. "Welcome back to the ranch," he said, resting his hands on her shoulder. Then he turned to Lauren and brushed a quick kiss over her cheek. "And good to see you, my dear."

"And you brought the groceries." Lauren gave him a quick hug. "Well done."

Vic placed a hand over his chest. "You know me. I have a servant heart."

Erin watched their casual give-and-take, thankfulness welling up at the sight. Lauren had had her own struggles, as well. Being left at the altar by a man she'd given so much of her life to had soured her on men. To see her so relaxed with Vic gave Erin a glimmer of hope for happy endings.

At least for her sisters. Herself, not so much.

Then Vic noticed Caitlin in Jodie's arms. "Well, well. Is there something I missed?" Vic joked, grinning at Jodie. "Something you want to tell me?"

His comment was meant in fun but shame flickered through Erin.

"Don't tell Finn." Jodie gave Vic a wink and then shot Erin a meaningful glance.

"She's my daughter," Erin said, the words echoing in the house. The same house that often held the condemning voice of their father, reminding the girls to behave. *Be good.*

And I was. I was always good, Erin told herself, clenching her hands, fighting down the disgrace she'd struggled with ever since she saw that plus sign on the home pregnancy kit.

Vic's puzzled stare just underlined her own shame. Then the porch door closed again, echoing in the silence that followed and Dean came into the room.

Don't see the man for twelve years and then twice in one day. Just her luck.

Dean's shadowed gaze ticked from her to her sisters as he set a couple of grocery bags on the counter, then the baby Jodie still held, then finally back to Erin. He gave her a quick nod. "Hey, again," he said, taking off his hat and dropping it beside the bags. "Didn't think you'd beat us here."

"I changed my mind about going to the Grill and Chill," she said.

His smile tightened and she wondered if he had hoped to arrive and leave before she came.

"So. You have a baby," Vic said, stating the obvious.

Erin took her from her sister, cradling her close. "I do. She's six weeks old and her name is Caitlin."

She didn't have to look at her sisters to read the questions that hovered ever since she'd thrust her daughter into their arms. She had been in and out of touch for the past half year and hadn't even come to their father's funeral. She had been on bed rest and couldn't travel.

But every time she picked up her phone to tell Jodie and Lauren, every time she wrote up a text to explain why, she'd gone with inane details instead. The truth would take hours and pages.

Plus she just couldn't deal with the inevitable questions about the circumstances and the baby's father.

"Do you guys want some coffee?" Jodie asked, her voice artificially bright.

"I'm good."

"Sure. That'd be nice."

Dean and Vic spoke at the same time then looked at each other. "We can stay for a while," Vic said, tilting his brother a questioning look.

Dean shook his head and Erin guessed he was about as comfortable around her as she was around him.

You'd think all those years would have eased the awkwardness, Erin thought, rocking Caitlin. It was as if she and Dean were back in those unwieldy high school years when emotions were heightened and judgments abounded.

But now, it felt as if the roles were reversed. She didn't know where Dean was at in his life, but she wasn't the girl she once was. The girl who thought herself too good for Dean Moore.

"I think we should let the sisters spend some time together," Dean said. "We should go."

Vic looked like he didn't want to agree.

"And I'm sure Lauren and Jodie want to get to know their niece," Dean added.

His voice held an odd tone and she shot a quick glance his way to figure out what he meant. But he wasn't looking at her.

She didn't know why that bothered her. It was like she wasn't there.

"Okay. We'll push off then," Vic said, giving Lauren another brief kiss. "I'll call you tonight."

Lauren's soft smile for Vic gave Erin a tinge of jealousy. She was happy for her sister. Happy her life had come to this good place. But it was hard not to wonder what her own future looked like.

Just before Dean left, his eyes drifted to Erin once more and for a heartbeat their gazes held.

She wasn't sure what to read into his enigmatic expression.

Didn't matter, she thought, cradling her head over Caitlin. She had other priorities and another focus.

Dean Moore's opinion of her wouldn't affect her at all.

"I should change Caitlin," Erin muttered, looking around for the diaper bag, as the guys left.

"Here's what you want," Lauren said, bending over and picking up the bag from where it lay beside Caitlin's car seat.

"I'll be right back," Erin said, once again retreating to the washroom. She didn't linger, however, and made quick work of changing her daughter's wet diaper. Caitlin's eyes were drawn to the lights above the sink and as she kicked her bare legs Erin felt again that wave of love. This tiny baby was so amazing.

"Love you so much," she whispered as she picked her fragile body up and held her close.

Lauren was pouring water into the coffeemaker when she came back and Jodie was putting together a plate of snacks. Cheese and crackers and cookies.

Her favorite white chocolate macadamia nut, from what Erin could see.

"Just go sit down," Lauren said, turning on the coffeemaker and then setting out some mugs.

Erin walked into the living room and dropped into the nearest couch, finally giving in to the weariness that had fuzzed her brains and dragged at her limbs. She leaned back into the chair as she cradled her now-quiet daughter in her arms, letting herself absorb the familiarity of this place. She knew Lauren and especially Jodie had resented coming here those summers of their youth, after their parents' divorce, but she'd always enjoyed it in spite of their taciturn father.

"You look tired," Jodie said as she brought the plate to the living room.

"I am. Been driving most of today. It's a good thing Caitlin was so well behaved for most of the trip."

She glanced around the room, then frowned as she noticed an empty space in one corner of the living area. "Did you sell your piano?"

"No. We moved it to Finn's place. A tuner was in Saddlebank to work on the church's piano so we thought we would take the opportunity to move and tune mine while he was around." Jodie sat down beside Erin, her hand reaching to touch Caitlin, now swathed in her linen blanket. "She's so perfect," she breathed, her finger trailing over her tender cheek.

Erin's throat tightened up. The words she had rehearsed all the way here now seemed pointless and superficial in the face of her sister's acceptance. Then Lauren sat down across from her, her hands clasped between her knees, her blond hair hanging loose around her classical features.

"You look amazing," she said to Lauren. "I think being engaged agrees with you. Congratulations, by the way. I'm happy for you. For both of you." Erin turned to Jodie, encompassing her younger sister in her congratulations as well. "I never thought a free spirit like you would end up marrying a sheriff."

Jodie released a light laugh. "Me, neither. Though Finn isn't a sheriff like Dad was. He's a deputy, but he's quitting in a year. Hoping to focus on horse training, which is his first love. I don't know if you remember him. He stayed with the Moores when his mother took off on him."

"Vaguely." Erin hadn't gotten too involved with many of the people in Saddlebank. When she was here, she had spent a lot of her time on the ranch walking in the hills, or riding. The ten months they lived in Knoxville, where their mother moved them after her parents' divorce, were always a dissonant time for her. While her sisters loved being in Knoxville, and disliked being on the ranch the two months a year they were sent here by their grandmother after their mom died, she was the opposite. Though their grandmother tried, Erin knew it must have been difficult for her to raise three grandchildren. Erin, of all the children, seemed to sense the tension more keenly than her sisters did.

So when they were shipped off to the ranch to be with their father, who reluctantly took them in, Erin found a peace that eluded her sisters. She would faithfully do the chores assigned to them by their father before he went off to his job as sheriff of Saddlebank County, then literally head to the hills with her sketchbook. She loved her time alone with her thoughts.

And her God.

She stopped reminiscing, turning to Lauren again. "Speaking of the Moores, I certainly didn't think a cowboy like Vic was your type, either. You always were so businesslike. So proper and—"

"Stick in the mud." Lauren laughed as she brushed her hair back from her face, gold hoops swinging from her ears. "You can say it. I was."

"That's not what I wanted to say," Erin objected. "I meant, you were always so focused and so self-disciplined."

"Qualities I get to apply to running Aunt Laura's flower shop right in Saddlebank now that she's retiring."

"I'm glad to hear you're taking it over," Erin said. "I have such good memories of that place."

"Her home and store was a sanctuary for us," Lauren said with a gentle sigh. "And we needed that from time to time. Though I think Jodie and I managed to find some peace the past few months. Since Dad died."

Erin felt it again. The tug of unmet expectations. The sorrow she'd felt when she heard her father had died and she couldn't come to the funeral.

"I'm so sorry I didn't come," she said, struggling once again with her shame. "I do want to visit his grave when we have a chance."

"We'll go there. On Sunday."

Which meant she was expected to attend church.

However she wasn't getting into that now. They had other things to discuss.

"He also wrote us each a letter when he found out he was dying," Jodie said, laying her hand on Erin's shoulder. "There's one for you, too. I found them in the house when I was cleaning up."

Erin looked down at Caitlin, wondering what their

straightlaced, overly strict father would have said about his first grandchild. Born out of wedlock.

And more.

"I'd like to read it. But later." She had to get through this first hurdle—trying to find a way to explain to her sisters what had happened to her.

"Yes. Later," Jodie agreed.

A beat of silence followed and Erin knew that while they had much to catch up on, her baby was, for lack of a better metaphor, the elephant in the room that could no longer be ignored.

"So, this is Caitlin, like I said before," she began, pleased her voice came out so steady. "She's six weeks old. I was on bed rest for two months before her birth. That's why I didn't come to Dad's funeral. I cut back on my graphic design work so I could focus on her." The words came out stilted. Cold. As if she related the events of someone else's life. "She was a Caesarean birth, which meant another few weeks of rest and taking it easy."

And another few weeks of putting off what she knew she had to have done many months earlier, when she discovered she was pregnant.

Tell her sisters.

It wasn't until she knew they weren't selling the ranch that she finally dared to return. Finally thought she might have a place to create a home for herself and her daughter.

And she knew exactly where that would happen.

"Oh, honey. You should have told us," Lauren said, hitting her directly in the guilt zone.

"I didn't know how to tell you I got pregnant." Erin cuddled Caitlin closer, fighting to maintain her composure, frustrated at the sorrow that threatened. She didn't want to feel sorry for herself. She had made her own choices and was living with the consequences. She didn't want Caitlin to even sense she might have regretted having her. "I didn't know where Jodie was living," she continued, swallowing down her tears. "You were dealing with the aftermath of Harvey leaving you days before your wedding. I knew how devastating that was for you so I didn't think you needed my troubles. I was trying to handle this on my own."

No one said anything as the grandfather clock ticked off the seconds, then boomed the hour.

"And now you're here." Jodie put her hand on Erin's shoulder. "I'm glad you came."

"I am, too." Erin gave her sister a careful smile. "Once I found out you girls weren't selling the ranch I felt like I had a place to come back to."

"It is your home," Lauren said. "Though, in our defense when we talked about selling it you said you didn't care either way."

"If you sold it, I would have figured something else out. But knowing this place was available to me. That I had a share in it..." She let the sentence trail off.

"You felt like you had a home," Jodie finished for her.

Erin nodded. "I know you girls didn't always like coming here over the summer, but for me it was comfortable."

"You and your long forays into melancholy," Lauren teased.

Erin laughed, thankful for the gentle return to lightness and comfort.

"And I'm going to ask the other awkward question,"

Jodie said, her hand still resting on Erin's shoulder. "Is Caitlin's father involved?"

Erin bit her lip trying to find the right way to tell them. "We aren't together anymore."

"Is he supporting you in any way?"

Was that a faintly chiding tone in Jodie's voice or was she being especially sensitive?

"He is not interested," she said firmly. "And I don't want to have anything more to do with him. It's…what we had…is over."

She was skating on the very edge of vague but her response and her vehemence seemed to satisfy her sisters. She simply couldn't deal with the past. She wanted to move forward into the new place she had found herself.

Caitlin stirred in her arms and Erin held her closer, as if protecting her. Too easily she recalled the look on Sam's face when she'd given him the news. She'd thought he would be happy. Thought he would finally make a decision about their relationship.

Instead the fury on his face and the check he wrote out to her to pay for an abortion had cut her to the core. And when she found out he was married already, her world tilted so far over she didn't think she would ever find her footing. She'd walked away and never contacted him again.

Now she was here and ready to look ahead and leave the past behind her.

"Well, you have us," Lauren said, leaning forward. "And you have a share in the ranch. Vic and I discussed the situation and he'll be talking to his banker about buying your third of the ranch out to give you some cash."

Erin knew she was entitled to a portion of the ranch and had already planned what she wanted. "The only thing I want is the Fletcher house. I want that to be my home."

"But, honey, you can stay here. In this house," Lauren said, sounding hurt.

"No. You and Vic will be living here. I don't want to be in the way."

Lauren didn't reply, which confirmed Erin's guess.

"We can figure out what the house and a few acres of it are worth and I'll take that as my share of the ranch." Erin looked down at Caitlin as a slow peace sifted over the chaos that had rocked her life for the past half year. "I just want a place of my own. A place I can be alone."

"That's fine and we can deal with the other details later on," Lauren agreed. "But the house you want to move into will need work."

"So I'll do it."

"You're a graphics designer, not a carpenter."

"I know a few things about building." Erin chuckled at her sister's incredulous look. "I learned a lot rehabbing the house my roommates and I lived in."

"Well, yes. You said that in some of your texts," Jodie agreed. "But—"

"You just can't imagine that your daydreaming sister can concentrate long enough to handle a skill saw. You should see some of the work I've done."

They hadn't of course. Jodie was running around, trying to find herself, playing piano in bars and looking for some kind of peace. Lauren was following her ex-fiancé Harvey around, looking for some kind of commitment.

All the while Erin had been looking for a home. A place to settle down and a man to settle down with. When she bought the house with her friends and started dating Sam she thought she'd found at least both.

She stopped her thoughts from heading down that dead-end road.

"At any rate, we should to talk to Jan Peter about this," Lauren insisted. "The local carpenter."

"Let me see the house first," Erin said. "I know moving in with you is the more practical option but I've been living on top of three roommates for the past year. If it'll work for me to live there while the work is going on, I don't mind."

"But what about Caitlin? Should you move her into the house?"

"We'll look at it first, then I'll decide for sure. But at this stage Caitlin tends to be oblivious to what's going on. Sleeps like a baby," she joked.

Erin didn't miss the sidelong glances Jodie and Lauren shared. Spacey Erin, making inappropriate jokes.

"I'll talk to Vic and Dean about it," Lauren said. "We could see what they say."

Erin knew staying in this house with Lauren was her best option but she couldn't shake the need for some quiet. For a place to put down some roots.

"Another thing, I'll need to get internet service up and running," she said. "I want to get working as soon as possible."

"Do you have work?"

Erin looked away from responsible Lauren to her younger sister Jodie who probably better understood that life could be erratic at times. That plans get messed up.

"I've just started up again." She glanced down at her

daughter. "I had…Caitlin and a few other things to deal with. But I've got a few bites on some feelers I put out."

"I'm sure you'll be back at it in no time." Jodie gave her a one-armed hug and leaned closer to Caitlin, cupping her tiny shoulder with one hand. "And now you've got help."

Erin felt tears threaten at the thought that she wasn't on her own anymore. But she wasn't going to let herself get pulled into the pity vortex. She had made her own choices. Made her own bed.

Now she had to lie in it.

Chapter Three

"So it looks like the basic structure is sound." Jan Peter looked around the inside of the house, pushing against a wall between the dining and living room. "The bearing walls are solid and if you're not knocking any of them out, we won't need to look at supporting beams."

Jan was a tall man with friendly eyes, graying mustache and a quiet air that hid the savvy businessman he really was. Dean followed him around, his uneven footsteps echoing in the empty space. He had to force himself to concentrate on what Jan was saying and not to look too hard at Erin who stood beside her sister in the living room, her baby cradled in her arms.

He would have preferred not to see her so soon after their first meeting, but his truck was still at Alan Brady's mechanic shop and wouldn't be ready until tomorrow, so Jan had picked him up today. Then, as they drove, he'd told Dean he had to stop at a job right on the way. It wasn't until they pulled into the yard that he discovered they were looking at the same house he had spun his own dreams around. When he and Tiffany were dating they would stop at this house, peek in the windows and plan.

Instead he was listening to his boss talking with Erin and Lauren about what they needed to do to make the house ready for the winter, and struggling with mixed feelings at her presence.

Today she wore blue jeans. Her hair looked tidier. She looked less weary and far more attractive.

"I just want to know if I can move in right away," Erin was asking.

"If we're not doing any interior work you can, but it'll be noisy," Jan said, turning back to Dean. "So what do you think we'll need to do? I know you've talked about fixing up this place yourself."

Dean was pleased that Jan asked his opinion. "The shingles on the roof are good but the siding should be redone," he said, remembering the changes he and Tiffany had talked about. "I'd replace the living room window—the seal is busted and it's all fogged up. Same with the one in the spare room upstairs."

"Spare room?" Jan slanted him a questioning look. "Which one is that?"

When he and Tiffany were making plans they had given each of the rooms a name. Master bedroom, first kid's room, second kid's room and spare room. But he wasn't about to admit that much in front of Erin.

"The smallest one," he said, hoping he sounded more nonchalant than he felt. "To your right when you go up the stairs."

"Did you live here?" Jan asked.

"No. I just been here before," Dean said, catching Erin's confusion as well in his peripheral vision.

He wasn't about to satisfy it, either. Bad enough

that she got to see him in all his crippled splendor, she definitely didn't need to hear about losing his dreams when Tiffany jilted him.

In favor of his brother.

"I think you're right about the work it needs." Jan turned to Erin. "The renos Dean suggested are the ones we have to do to get the house ready for winter. We'll pick a warm day to replace the windows. You won't be cold, but you might be fighting flies that day." Jan grinned at Erin but she was looking around, a peculiar smile on her face, as if the idea of living here held infinite appeal.

Dean knew how she felt. He was thirty-three and still living at home. That definitely hadn't been in his ten-year plan. When his brother started renting the ranch from Keith he had hoped to get this place subdivided. This house had been his goal.

"So I could live here? Right away?" Erin asked.

Jan shrugged, brushing off the dust he'd gathered while inspecting the attic. "You could move in this afternoon if you want. Like I said, you'll have to put up with a few inconveniences when we do the windows."

"That's good news."

Jan turned to Dean. "I'm putting you on this job. If you need help I might be able to spare a guy here and there but for the most part I think you can do this on your own."

"I thought I would be helping on that new barn you're building by Mercy." He didn't want to work on this house. He didn't want Erin to see him making his slow and methodical way up and down a ladder or scaffolding.

And the fact that it bothered him, well, that bothered him, too. He wasn't supposed to care what people thought of him. He was Dean Moore. A tough-as-leather cowboy and, even more, a saddle bronc rider.

One-time bronc rider, his thoughts taunted him.

"Isn't there someone else who can do this work?"

Erin's question caught Dean off guard, though he shouldn't have been surprised. Clearly she didn't think he could do the job, either.

"Dean's capable," Jan said. The faint narrowing of Jan's eyes encouraged Dean though it would take a lot more than a bit of restrained anger on the part of his boss to balance out Erin's lack of confidence.

"I wasn't thinking of that," Erin said, lifting one hand, clearly flustered. "It's just… I thought…" She waved off her comments. "I'm sure Dean is more than able to do the work."

"Good. I think so, too, otherwise I wouldn't have put him on the job."

"Look, if this is going to be a problem, let me work on that job in Mercy," Dean said.

Jan slowly shook his head, gnawing at one corner of his mouth, a sure sign he had something he didn't really want to say. "Sorry, I just hired on a new guy and he's married and got a couple of kids. He needs the hours. Besides, this is close by and I won't have to charge out traveling time for you." Jan gave him a careful smile, as if hoping that would placate him. "And this way you can start whenever you want. Work your own hours."

It all sounded so reasonable, but his boss's comments still bothered him. And he was trying hard not to read subtext in his reasoning. Working his own hours meant flexibility for the rehab he was supposed to be doing and for the days he wasn't well because the pain took over.

"Of course," he said. "I get it."

Then his eyes slid sideways to where Erin stood. She was looking at him and he didn't imagine the pity on her face.

Anger surged through him. Anger with his circumstances and that Erin had to be a witness to this moment.

He wasn't good enough. Simple as that. Just a washed-up bronc rider who couldn't even get on a horse.

Erin hadn't wanted anything to do with him all those years ago. He was convinced she certainly wouldn't want anything to do with him now.

"Be it ever so humble." Lauren turned off the vacuum cleaner and looked around the living room with a half smile. They had been busy in Erin's new house most of yesterday and today, cleaning and moving furniture in.

"It looks homey," Erin said, pushing a brown leather recliner into the corner beside the rust-colored couch Lauren had just finished cleaning. A wooden table replete with scuff marks and coffee rings sat in front if it. Mismatched end tables flanked the couch, each holding different lamps. A love seat in a pink plaid sat across from the couch. They had come out of a storage shed on Vic's mom's place. The rest came from the second-hand store in Saddlebank.

Two wooden chairs and three folding chairs were tucked under the oval wooden table in the dining room. A metal watering can holding daisies and lilies sat on the table. That particular touch of whimsy was courtesy of Jodie, who had shown up only briefly, full of apologies. She and Finn had a last-minute meeting with Abby Bannister to scout out some wedding photo locations.

It didn't matter to Erin that Jodie couldn't be here. She would see her again. That much she could count on now that she was back at the ranch.

"It's perfect," Erin said, folding her arms as she glanced around the room. Her home.

Her own.

And the best part was the cast-iron wood stove taking up the far corner of the living room. She already could imagine being curled up on the couch, reading a book, Caitlin in her arms, the lights low as a fire crackled in the stove.

"And you're sure about this?" Lauren was asking as she plumped the pillows they had found at the bargain store in Mercy. "You're sure about living here on your own?"

"Believe it or not, I am," Erin said. "You have no idea what a treat it will be for me to have my own office."

"Vic said the internet people might be coming tomorrow so it will be a day or two before you're connected again."

"That's okay. I'll need a couple of days to get myself organized."

"Will you be able to keep busy? Out here?"

Erin chuckled at the skepticism in her sister's voice. "I actually just got a call this morning from a previous client in Colorado. He wants me to do a series of static and interactive graphics for his website and some promotional material he will be putting out. It won't be for a month or so but in the meantime I've got a few feelers out on some other work."

Lauren shot her a puzzled look. "Still can't believe all that coloring and sketching you used to do has translated into a job."

"The degree in graphics design probably helped, too."

"Of course." Lauren gave her a smile, then dropped the pillows on the couch. "So this is the last of it. I'm really glad we managed to find a crib for Caitlin, as well. At least she won't have to sleep in an apple box."

"Or a bottom drawer of a dresser like Granny always said Mom did," Erin said with a laugh.

Lauren released a gentle sigh, glancing down at the engagement ring on her finger then over at Erin. "I've been thinking about Mom lately, what with so many changes in our lives. Jodie getting married, me engaged. And now you with the first—" She stopped there as if not sure what to say.

"The first grandchild," Erin finished for her. "I've been thinking about Mom, too. And Dad. I know I've said it already, but I'm sorry I missed the funeral."

Lauren gave her sister a quick hug. "You had your reasons. Did you read Dad's letter to you?"

"I haven't had a chance. Caitlin was fussy most of last night."

"You should have woken me or Jodie up," Lauren chided, giving her shoulders a gentle shake. "Either of us would gladly have held her."

Erin felt a surprising hitch to her heart. The six weeks she'd spent at the house with her roommates after Caitlin was born had been fraught with tension.

Though her friends were helpful and for the most part considerate, she still overheard muted grumbling about short nights and interrupted sleep. She wasn't accustomed to having help offered.

"Sorry. I didn't think—"

"That Jodie or I would want to hold our own niece?" Lauren shook her head. "Honey, you're with family. You're allowed to have expectations."

Which was probably part of her problem with Sam, Erin figured. She didn't dare have expectations. Each time she brought up their future he would gently tell her she shouldn't pressure him. They would talk later.

Then later came and here she was.

"Speaking of," Lauren said, tilting her head, "I think I hear something."

Erin heard a squawk from the room she'd claimed as her bedroom and was about to go get Caitlin when Lauren stopped her.

"I'll do this. You just sit down."

Then she hurried off.

But Erin wasn't about to sit down. Not with the bags of stuff they had purchased sitting on counters. She was eager to put it away. To get her kitchen cleaned up and organized.

Just then Dean came into the house carrying a box holding her laptop and router and Erin was distracted by a more important task.

"Here. Let me," she said.

"I got this." He shot her an annoyed glance.

"I don't mind helping," she said, reaching out to take the box from him.

As she did her hands brushed his and they both

pulled back at the same time. Which made the box tilt precariously.

Dean shifted and took a sudden step left. In the process he fell against the recliner, which teetered as Dean struggled to regain his footing.

Erin made another grab for the box, but Dean caught his balance, grimacing as he did.

"Are you okay?" she asked, concerned at his quick intake of breath.

"I'm fine. Leave me alone."

"I'm sorry. It's just that's my laptop in that box. I need it for my work and I didn't want—"

"Didn't want it to fall?" Dean gave her a sardonic look and handed her the box. "Here. Take it if you think I'll drop it."

She wanted to protest, realizing she had overreacted. She wanted to explain that the laptop was new. That she still owed money on it. That she needed it for her job. A job she now needed more than ever since she had Caitlin depending on her and she had medical bills to pay.

But that would have taken too many words and too much exposing of her life to someone she preferred to keep in her past.

Then she looked up at him and was dismayed to see him staring at her as he still clung to the box. They stood there, old memories braiding through the moment. How intense he could be the times he asked her out. How her foolish heart had beat just a little faster each time he did. How her practical mind told her to say no.

Then he gave the box a tiny shove, returning it to her. But as she took it, she felt as if he was also pushing her away.

She shook her head as she set it on the kitchen table, suddenly disoriented. It bothered her that a simple touch of Dean's hands created such a strong reaction in her.

Then Lauren came out of the room holding Caitlin and reality settled her faintly beating heart.

She had a daughter to take care of. She had responsibilities. Her reaction to Dean was just a hearkening back to old memories. With all that had happened to her in the past, she knew she was stronger than that.

She had to be.

The next morning, Dean parked his truck and shot a quick glance at his watch. 7:45. He couldn't see any movement inside the house. Maybe he had come too early?

Not that it mattered anymore. The growl of the diesel engine coming on the yard would have woken Erin up.

The house was tucked into a copse of trees and as he got out of the truck the wind picked up, rustling through the leaves of the aspen. They were already showing a tinge of orange and yellow amongst the green. Fall was on the way, but thankfully today was warmer.

He walked to the back of his truck and opened the tailgate. The ladder he needed to unload was long and unwieldy and he would have to do some creative lifting to get it to the house.

As he manhandled it out of the truck, he felt a strong twinge in his leg followed by one of regret. Jan had offered to come by and help him get everything ready, but after Erin expressed her doubts about his ability he wanted to prove he could do it himself.

The end of the ladder came off the truck and crashed to the ground. Next step was getting it to the house.

"Do you a need a hand?"

Dean's heart jumped and he spun around, almost unbalancing himself in the process.

Erin walked toward him, her baby tucked in some kind of carrier strapped to her front.

She wore a long sweater that flowed as she walked. Her hair was tied up in a loose bun-looking thing emphasizing her narrow features. And once again he wondered what had happened to her the past few years to put that edge in her voice, that hardness in her eyes, the hollows in her cheeks. Wondered if it had anything to do with the baby she carried.

"I'm okay," he said, lifting his chin as if challenging her to help him. "I do this for a living."

"I'll let you get to your work. But let me know if you need a hand."

He just nodded, glancing from her face to the baby bundled against her chest. "I doubt you'll be able to help much."

"Excuse me," she huffed, sounding insulted. "I know how to handle a hammer and nails. I've done home renovations before."

Her snippy tone was a shock. "So tell me, Miss Home Renovations, why is it okay for you to question my abilities but not okay for me to question yours?"

She looked taken aback. "What do you mean?"

So now she was going to play dumb. Tiffany had excelled at that. Throwing back his suspicions about her faithfulness by going on the defensive and lobbing out questions.

He wanted to make it easy for both of them and drop it. But if he was working here for the next week or so, he needed to face her doubts head-on. "Tuesday, when Jan and I were here, you asked if there was someone else who could do the work. Like you didn't think I was capable."

She blushed, which did two things. Confirmed his suspicions and made him even angrier.

"I may not be able to ride a bucking bronc, but I can fix your siding and replace your windows," he said, wishing he could keep the anger out of his voice. Seeing his ex-girlfriend's pitying look just before she dumped him had been a tough pill to swallow. Going through the slow and painful steps of rehab even more so. But to have this girl whom he once admired and dreamed of dating treat him like less of a man was like a slap. "It might take me longer than usual and if that's a worry, I'll tell Jan to adjust your bill," he snapped. "Call it a disability discount."

Erin took a step back, looking as if he had hit her and he regretted being so defensive.

"I'm sorry" was all she said. Then she turned and strode back to the house, her sweater flaring behind her in her hurry to get away from him.

He blew out a sigh as she closed the door, shaking his head at his stupid outburst. *Way to go, Moore*, he chided himself. Way to treat the customer.

She was probably in the house, calling Jan up and telling him she didn't want this crazy man on her yard anymore.

He sucked in a breath and picked up one end of the

ladder, pulling it away from the truck. Then he started toward the house, his steps deliberate as he dragged the thing behind him.

He hoped she didn't look out the window at this point to see just how disabled he really was. He knew it shouldn't matter to him what she thought.

But it did. Far too much.

As he lifted the ladder against the house, moving slowly and carefully, he struggled with his own doubts.

He would finish up here today and then he would phone Jan and tell him he had to find someone else.

No way was he going to work for someone who didn't think he could do the job.

Especially not Erin McCauley.

Chapter Four

Erin drizzled the glaze on the bundt cake she had made, then stood back to admire her handiwork.

Too much? Not enough?

What kind of cake did you bake for the man in front of whom you'd made a complete fool of yourself? What kind of cake said "I'm sorry" the best?

This morning, after her run-in with Dean, she had packed up Caitlin and made a quick trip to town to talk to the people at Dis-Connected about getting her internet up and running. From there she'd headed to the grocery store to pick up a few things she was missing, as well as supplies to bake this cake.

But now that it was done she was having second thoughts. Should have just gone with cookies. Or muffins.

She tossed the bowl with the remainder of the icing into the sink. Seriously, how indecisive could she be? Had Sam done this to her? Stolen her identity and her confidence?

The answer to that would be a resounding yes if she were honest with herself. But she didn't want to admit he'd had that much influence in her life. Lauren had always accused her of being a people pleaser. Her life with Sam was the epitome of that personality trait.

She could hear Dean clattering around outside, going up and down the ladder. She didn't know what he was doing out there, only that she wasn't going out to watch. After his outburst she doubted he would appreciate spectators.

Well, the cake was done and it was a quarter to twelve. He would be quitting for lunch soon. Perfect time to bring it out to him.

She glanced at the clock again just as her phone rang.

It was Jodie.

"Hey, sweetie," Jodie trilled, "I'm about five minutes away. Can I stop in?"

"Of course. You're always welcome here."

"I kind of figured, but I don't want to intrude."

Jodie's words gave her a tick of sorrow. In her shame and retreat from her sisters had she come across as so unapproachable?

"Will Caitlin be awake?" Jodie asked.

"She's sleeping now, but I'm sure she'll be up soon." Thankfully Caitlin had settled in last night. It was as if she too sensed they had arrived at their final destination.

This morning Erin had gone for a walk around the property and down the road, just to get a sense of the place. To let herself enjoy the space, the quiet and the simple fact that this belonged to her and only her.

Then she'd made a fool of herself in front of Dean.

"Then if it's okay, I'm coming over," Jodie said.

"That would be great."

This way she could put off the agony of indecision over the cake she had just made and, instead, catch up with Jodie. She wanted to talk about the wedding and settle back into her sister's life. The easier sister's life.

Though she and Lauren were twins, she always felt like the younger sister around her. She knew Lauren loved her, but the dismayed expression on Lauren's face when she'd arrived with Caitlin showed Erin how disappointed her twin was.

Whereas Jodie's reaction had been one of joy.

Erin set the cake aside, quickly washed up the dishes she had used, tidying with a sense of anticipation. She shot a glance around the house. Everything was in order.

Outside she could hear thumps and the occasional screech of nails. She was very curious as to what he was doing, but her embarrassment over how he had misinterpreted their last interaction kept her inside the house, uselessly tidying. Then she heard a muffled squawk from the bedroom and she rushed to pick up her daughter. Just as she came out of the room she heard a vehicle pull up.

And as Jodie came up the cracked and uneven sidewalk, carrying a bouquet of flowers, Erin's throat thickened and tears welled up in her eyes.

She opened the door and Jodie hurried toward her, arms wide.

"Hey, sis," Erin managed as Jodie grabbed her in a careful hug.

Jodie held her close, Caitlin snuggled between them as tears spilled.

"Oh, honey," Jodie murmured, rocking her back and forth. "It's been a long road for you, I think."

Erin sniffed, annoyed at how easily she cried in front of her sister, yet thankful for someone whom she felt comfortable enough around to do exactly that.

Jodie pulled back and smoothed Erin's tears away with the balls of her thumbs, her expression sympathetic. "You're home, you know."

"I know. I think that's why I'm feeling so weepy."

"And you just had a baby."

"That, too," Erin said with a tremulous laugh.

"So, you take these and I'll take her," Jodie said, handing Erin the flowers while she carefully removed Caitlin from Erin's arms, cradling her as they walked into the house.

Jodie sat down on the couch and bent over her niece, inhaling slowly. "Oh, my goodness. She smells so sweet." She rubbed her nose over Caitlin's tiny one. "And you are such an amazing gift. You are, you know," she cooed to Caitlin. "You are a perfect little gift to our family. We're so blessed to have you."

Erin felt the bonds of guilt and shame that had held her soul loosen at Jodie's simple, accepting words.

"By the way, Lauren and Aunt Laura both say hi, hence the flowers," Jodie said indicating the bouquet Erin was cutting the ends off of. "They both wanted to come, but they both have to work whereas self-employed me can take time off and have you and Caitlin all to myself," she said, her head tilting slightly as she heard the sound of hammering. "So I noticed Dean's here already?"

"Yeah. He came this morning," Erin said, removing the fake flowers Jodie had brought yesterday from the metal watering can and filling it with water. "And now I've got this apology cake cooling on the counter that I don't know what to do with."

"Apology cake? Never heard of that recipe," Jodie said, frowning her puzzlement.

"Well, it's about a cup of my-big-mouth, mixed in with three tablespoons of wounded pride and a soup-çon of McCauley."

"Oooooh, that cake," Jodie said with a knowing nod of her head. "I should have baked a few of those in my life. That and Humble Pie." Then she shot her a questioning glance. "So I'm guessing the cake is for Dean?"

"Oh, yeah."

"What did you say to him?"

Erin set the flowers in the pot and put it back on the table, avoiding her sister's gaze. "I kind of made it sound like he wasn't capable of fixing my house. At least I think he took it that way."

"Oh, dear."

"It wasn't that I thought he couldn't do it," she said, fiddling with the flowers, arranging them just so. "It's just, well, I'm not comfortable being around him and my mouth got away on me."

"Honey, that's my line, not yours."

"I know. I was feeling weird."

Weird and ashamed. She had always been the good girl. The one who turned down Dean's many requests for dates because he was too rough and rowdy for her. Now she was the one who wasn't "suitable." She was the one who had messed up her life.

"Anyhow, I felt bad so I thought I would bake him a cake," Erin continued.

"I should go get him so we can eat it. He's probably

not had lunch yet." She shot her sister a questioning glance as she stood. "If that's okay with you?"

"I guess." Dean would be working here so she figured she might as well try to smooth things over between them as soon as possible.

Jodie walked to the door still carrying her baby.

"I'll take Caitlin, though," Erin said, holding out her arms for her daughter.

"I'll be careful."

Erin held Jodie's puzzled gaze for a beat, surprised at the flutter of panic that seeing Jodie walk away with her daughter created in her. "I know. It's just... I haven't had anyone else taking care of her since she was born. Besides, she needs her diaper changed."

Jodie seemed to understand and handed Caitlin over to Erin, but as she did she held Erin's eyes. "Are you okay?"

"I'm fine," she said, disappointed at how breathless she sounded, glancing down at Caitlin. "I'm just fine."

"Okay, I'll be inside shortly."

Then Jodie disappeared around the side of the house.

Erin took a steadying breath, her heart finally slowing down. What was wrong with her? Why the panic attack? This was her sister, not some random stranger.

Hormones. That's what she was blaming it on, she reasoned, cuddling Caitlin closer as she walked toward her bedroom.

A few moments later she had Caitlin's diaper changed and her baby lay swaddled up in a bouncy chair Lauren had rustled up from some of the cousins. Caitlin stared, cross-eyed, at the little stuffed animals hanging from the bar straddling the chair, her mouth a perfect little O.

As Erin held her daughter's tiny fingers, wrapped tightly around her own, her heart pinched.

Would it ever get old? she thought, marveling at the delicacy of her fingernails, the delicate swath of her thick eyelashes.

"You didn't get those from me," she murmured, brushing her finger over her baby's cheek. Unbidden thoughts of Caitlin's father entered her mind and behind that came the ever-present shame and guilt. "I didn't know," she whispered to her baby. "I just didn't know."

"I'm too busy to stop," Dean grumbled, yanking on a piece of the siding and tossing it to the side to join the pile already there.

"You have to eat lunch some time," Jodie said, looking up at him perched up on the ladder, her hands planted on her hips.

Dean ignored both her and the grumbling of his stomach at the thought of lunch. He was hungry, but he wasn't about to get down the ladder in front of Jodie. He inserted his claw hammer under the next nail.

"I packed a lunch" was all he said. "I'll eat it when it works."

"Then come and eat it with us," she said, slipping a wayward strand of hair behind her ear. "Erin made a cake. She called it an apology cake. Not sure what that meant, but I think she feels bad about something she did or said to you."

Dean couldn't help the flush warming his neck. Erin's doubts about his ability had fueled most of the work he'd done this morning. Had made him push himself harder than he probably should have.

But the fact that she felt sorry tweaked his ego just

enough. That and the fact that his leg was on fire and he really could use a break.

"Give me about five minutes and I'll come inside."

"You got 'er," Jodie said with a quick salute. He waited until she was around the corner of the house before he worked his awkward way to the ground, fighting his frustration at each halting step.

His physiotherapist had warned him that it would take time and to be careful. Not that he'd spent that much time with Mike the past couple of months. Mike had called Dean a few times, but Dean had ignored the calls. Every time he went it was like he was reminded again of how useless he was and he hated asking Jan for time off work to make the appointments.

Dean stopped at the bottom of the ladder. He massaged his aching leg, stretching it out, still debating the wisdom of going into the house. Then he heard Jodie calling him and he knew he couldn't put it off any longer.

With a sigh he brushed the sawdust and dirt off his shirt and pants and walked through the overgrown grass to his truck. He grabbed the thermos of coffee he'd made this morning and grimaced at the sight of the plastic grocery bag holding his lunch. A couple of peanut butter sandwiches and some homemade cookies. He'd had a few good-natured battles over this with his mother when he started working for Jan. She'd wanted to make his lunch, accusing him of not packing nutritious food.

Well, she was right. But there was no way, on top of still living at home, that he was letting him mom pack his lunch, too. That was too many shades of pathetic.

He took his time going down the uneven sidewalk

on his way to the house from the truck. His legs were still shaky from the exertion of going up and down the ladder and the last thing he needed was a stumble. He'd have to call Jan tonight and ask if he could get some scaffolding instead. The siding would be more work than he thought.

He paused just inside the door of Erin's house, his eyes adjusting from the bright light outside.

Erin stood with her back to him, stirring something on the stove. Soup, he guessed from the mouth-watering smell.

"There you are. I thought you were ducking out on us," Jodie called out, carrying some bowls to the table.

"No. Just getting my lunch," he said as he toed his boots off.

Jodie gave a pointed look at the plastic bag he carried. "That's what you're eating?"

"Proudly homemade," he said, waving it aloft, grinning at her. He'd spent enough time with Jodie over the past few months that he felt at ease with her.

Then Erin turned and her eyes grazed over him as she brought the pot to the table.

He wished it didn't bother him. Wished he could be as casual around her as he was around Jodie.

He glanced around as he set his bag on the table. He couldn't see Caitlin and figured she was sleeping.

"So, this is nice," Jodie said, grinning from him to Erin like they were all one happy family. "Like old times."

Dean wasn't precisely sure which old times Jodie referred to, but from her overly bright smile he sensed she was trying hard to make everyone comfortable.

"Where do you want me to sit?" Dean asked.

"By that sad little lunch you packed and may as well save for your dog, Lucky," Jodie returned, grabbing a bowl and filling it up. "We have real food. I brought bread from the bakery and soup from the Grill and Chill. George was right ticked when I asked him if it was fresh. Got all grumpy Gus on me. Honestly, not sure what Brooke sees in him."

"Are they dating now?" Erin asked, finally speaking up, but looking at Jodie as she asked about the couple who had been off and on as long as Dean knew them.

"That's the rumor. There have been a few George and Brooke sightings ever since the concert this spring. I have stopped holding my breath when it comes to that relationship. But then, who knows how the heart works. I never thought I would end up with Finn or Lauren with Vic."

While she chattered away Erin brought a plate of sandwiches to the table. They looked ten times better than the flattened and misshapen ones resting in the bag beside the bowl of soup Jodie had given him.

"I think we can start," Jodie said as she sat down directly across the table from Dean leaving Erin to sit either on his left or his right.

"Shall we pray?" Jodie asked brightly, holding her hand out to Erin who took it and, in what Dean could only assume was an automatic gesture, held her other hand out to him.

As soon as she realized what she had done, she blushed and snatched her hand back.

"What, you don't want to hold Dean's hand?" Jodie teased, as if trying to eradicate the sudden awkwardness. "He doesn't bite."

"Are you going to pray?" Erin asked, her voice holding a slight edge completely at odds with the girl Dean once knew.

"Sure. Sorry." Jodie flashed her and Dean a smile, then bowed her head. "Thank You, Lord, for this food. For the blessing of family. Be with Erin and Caitlin as they make their new home here. Thank you that they are back here with us. Bless our work this afternoon. Amen."

Dean murmured an automatic amen which netted him a puzzled glance from Erin.

He knew how it looked to her. He'd always been the wild and crazy one laughing at her for going to church, mocking her faith even while part of him admired her quiet fortitude.

Well, people changed, as Kelly had so eloquently stated the other day on Main Street. And he found himself wanting to apologize for all the times he'd teased her about being a Bible thumper.

But not here and not now.

"So, how are things looking on the house?" Jodie asked, as if determined to make conversation.

"It's going to need more work than we initially thought." Dean blew on his soup and gave Erin an apologetic look. "So it's going to cost more than you might have figured on."

"That's okay," she said. "This is going to be our home. I want it to be sound."

"The ranch will cover the costs anyhow," Jodie assured him. "So don't worry about that."

"In that case…" He flashed Jodie a grin, trying not to let the tension around the table get to him.

"Let's not get carried away," she warned.

"So, no addition with a brick fireplace and stained-glass windows?"

"This is a house, not a church."

"According to my mom, God is as much present in a family gathering as a church one."

Dean laughed and once again he caught a puzzled look from Erin.

Okay, so maybe he was laying it on a bit thick, chatting with Jodie like he wasn't totally aware of Erin sitting beside him shooting him covert glances with those slate-blue eyes of hers. Acting like he and Jodie were best buddies when they'd just gotten to know each other better the past couple of months.

"How did Caitlin sleep last night?" Jodie asked Erin, drawing her sister into the conversation.

"Good. I think she was still tired from the drive on Monday." Erin stirred her soup and gave Jodie a tight smile. "It was a long trip."

Dean heard a note of sorrow in her voice, wondering precisely what caused it.

"You drove all the way up from San Francisco?" he asked.

She nodded, shooting him a quick glance.

"So what were you doing there?" As if he didn't know exactly what had kept her occupied all these years. Because somehow in spite of Tiffany, in spite of all the girls between then and now, she always hung, like a painting, in the back of his mind. Elusive and mysterious.

"Working as a graphic designer."

He wanted to ask her more and fill in the gaps between the last time he saw her and now. Wanted to know what had put those shadows under the eyes of the sweet, innocent girl who had turned him down one last time with a sad smile. A girl who'd told him he had to turn his life around.

Well, he had. Just too late for her, he guessed.

Chapter Five

"Thanks for the cake. It was delicious," Dean said, making a move to push his chair away from the table. "But I should get to work."

Erin wondered if she should tell him the story behind the cake. But sitting beside him at the table made her far too aware of him and apologizing would only exacerbate that. When Jodie had offered to pray and he had neither mocked nor teased her, she felt as if the earth had shifted beneath her.

He used to laugh at her faith. Call her Thumper, as in Bible thumper. But now, it seemed, the tables had truly turned.

"Do you need a hand?" she asked as she got up.

His angry frown told her that the apology cake hadn't taught her enough of a lesson.

"Like I said, I know how to handle a hammer," she retorted, determined to fight the self-conscious feelings he created in her. "I don't want to just sit around while you're working."

"It's okay," he said, seemingly placated by her response. "I've just got the one ladder. I'm going to call Jan to come with a scaffold tomorrow."

"You shouldn't be working so soon after having a baby, anyway," Jodie warned Erin. "Especially after a Caesarean."

"It's been almost two months," Erin said. "I won't be able to do any of my other work until I get the internet connection up and running. I need to do something."

The two months of bed rest and the exhaustion that claimed her after Caitlin's birth had been difficult enough to endure. She wanted to stay busy. To keep thoughts of the future at bay and the fear that could clutch her at times.

But you're home now.

"I'll let you know if I need a hand," Dean said, his tone brusque as he grabbed the bag holding his lunch.

Erin guessed he wouldn't, but didn't bother challenging him. She'd find something else to keep herself busy. Something she could do inside the house.

"Thanks again for lunch. It was good." He held up his bag. "Good thing I made this myself. My mom might be insulted if I fed this to my dog."

"I just hope Lucky isn't insulted," Jodie retorted. "Of course he's still a pup and thinks everything you do and everything you give him is amazing."

Erin was surprised at her flush of jealousy at the easy give-and-take between Jodie and Dean. At one time Jodie wasn't so accepting of him. She and Lauren had consistently warned her against him, as if she needed reminding of his unsuitability.

Now Jodie and Dean chatted away like brother and sister and for some reason it bothered her. She felt like she was on the outside looking in.

But just before he left his eyes caught hers and once again she felt it. That dangerous thrum Dean could always create in her.

Trouble was, while she'd resisted it then because he was unsuitable, she resisted it now for an entirely different reason.

The door closed behind him and Erin felt like she could breathe again.

"Cake was really good," Jodie said as she helped her clean up. "But you forgot to tell Dean why you made it."

"It seemed redundant" was all she said.

"It could have helped things along." Jodie put the bowls in the sink and started filling it with water. "He'll be working here for a few weeks. It would help if he knew you were okay with him being here."

Unfortunately she wasn't.

"He's had a tough go." Jodie turned to Erin, still holding the soap bottle. "And while I know we were kind of down on him when he was younger, he's not the same guy he used to be. The accident really changed him. So did him getting dropped by Tiffany."

Erin needed to deflect and dodge right about now. The last thing she needed was to hear Dean's praises sung. The irony of their situation wasn't lost on her. Instead she grasped at what Jodie had said.

"Dean was dating Tiffany Elders?" Tiffany was the kind of girl Erin used to be marginally jealous of. Pretty, confident and comfortable chatting up any guy she met.

"For a while. But she broke up with Dean just before his accident, hoping to get together with Vic again. She broke his heart."

"Vic's?"

"No. Dean's."

Erin wasn't sure why the thought of Dean nursing a broken heart over someone like Tiffany bothered her. "Sounds like a soap opera," she said picking up a dish towel to dry the dishes Jodie was washing up. "First one brother, then the other."

"I guess. But Dean's better off without her and Vic feels the same way. She was just trouble bouncing from one guy to the other. Last I heard she was in Colorado dating some married guy." Jodie shook her head as condemnation and guilt curled in Erin's stomach.

"I think I hear Caitlin," she murmured dropping her dish towel and hurrying to the bedroom. She closed the door behind her and leaned against it. As she did a far-too-familiar prayer rose up.

Forgive me, Lord.

She fought down the habitual pain and humiliation, wondering if she could ever feel like her life was on the right track.

But she was home now and had a chance at a new start.

She walked over to her daughter's crib, her heart melting at the sight of Caitlin's perfect features, her chubby little fingers curled up, her hand resting beside her head. A wave of love washed over her, so intense and overpowering it nearly toppled her. But, always behind that, came the slithering feeling that she didn't deserve this baby or her love.

"I'm sorry," she whispered, stroking Caitlin's head, fighting down unwelcome tears. "I do love you and I will take care of you to the best of my ability."

She bent over and brushed a kiss over her tender skin, cupped her head in her hand. Caitlin sighed, shook her head, then drifted back into sleep.

As Erin straightened she saw Dean walking slowly back to the house from his truck. Instead of going around the other side, he walked directly toward her window. He looked up and their eyes held. Then he gave her a curt nod and moved on.

"Everything okay?" she heard Jodie call out.

Erin gave her daughter one more kiss, then returned to the kitchen and her sister's company.

"We're fine," she said.

They finished doing the dishes and Jodie stayed a while longer before she left. That afternoon the internet company finally came and installed her wireless network and Erin was able to connect with her clients.

Her inbox tinged for about fifteen minutes as she scrolled through her email, deleting offers from graphics sites she subscribed to and various other businesses, and skimmed through a couple of letters from her former roommates checking to see how she was doing. She shifted them into another mailbox to reply to later.

Then her heart jumped as she saw an all-too-familiar name crop up in her inbox. Sam Sibley.

She immediately sent it to trash, emptied it and then blocked him. She didn't want to read anything he had to say. They were done.

The rest of the day was spent working on her latest project, but the entire time Sam's deleted email hovered in the dark recesses of her mind.

Consequently she ended up working late into the night knowing she wouldn't be able to sleep anyway.

Someone was trying to get in the house.

Someone was trying to get Caitlin, and Erin couldn't

get to her. She was outside and Caitlin was in the house. Crying.

Sam was in the bedroom. Sam was here to take her baby.

Erin panicked, yanking at the door to the bedroom, but it was stuck. Caitlin's cries grew louder. More desperate as Erin struggled to get to her daughter. It was as if her legs were tied together and she was swimming against an invisible current that pulled her back.

Her heart thundered in her chest as she fought against the implacable force. She had to get Caitlin. Sam was taking her away.

"Erin. Erin." Someone was calling her name through her daughter's cries.

She couldn't see who it was.

"Erin. Wake up."

The voice pierced the gloom surrounding her and she surged upward and into bright, blinding light.

She glanced around the unfamiliar room. Where was her baby? Where was she?

Living room. On the couch. She scrambled to her feet, blinking away the sleep that fogged her vision and just about fell over as her legs gave way.

But then an arm caught her and held her up.

"Hey. Erin. Are you okay?"

The voice was familiar and Erin struggled to get her mind to catch up, to wake up.

Slowly she became conscious of where she was. What was happening?

Dean stood beside her, holding her up. His eyes were focused on her and he was frowning. She held his gaze, trying to figure out what was going on. Then her eyes shifted and her heart jumped.

Caitlin was cradled in his other arm and she wasn't crying anymore.

Erin sucked in a breath, fighting to catch her balance, too aware of the fact that she leaned against Dean, his arm around her warm and strong.

She tried to pull away, but he wouldn't let her.

"I'll take her," she said.

"Just sit down and I'll give her to you. You're still half asleep." Erin struggled to fight him off, but she was still disoriented and couldn't get her bearings.

"My baby," she called out, reaching out for Caitlin.

"I'll give her to you just as soon as you're sitting down."

She obeyed and true to his word as soon as she was back down on the couch, he nestled Caitlin in her arms. Erin pulled her close, her panicked heart finally slowing down. But as soon as she relaxed she became aware that Dean still had his hand on her shoulder. For a moment she felt a sense of protection. Of being watched over.

But slowly reality intruded and she pulled herself back.

"I'm sorry," Dean said, straightening. "I heard her crying and she wouldn't stop and I thought maybe something happened to you. So I came in and she was alone in the crib."

Erin's heart slowed, but behind the receding fear came the crash of guilt as she held her daughter close. How could she have been so irresponsible? What if it wasn't Dean who had come in?

She took a breath, willed her racing heart to slow as she stared down at Caitlin, as if to make sure she was really lying quietly, now in her arms.

"I'm sorry. I was just worried about you," Dean continued. "Are you okay?"

She nodded, then finally dared to look up at him. "Yeah. I'm fine. I guess I fell asleep here."

His eyes on her looked kind. Caring. And again she felt an unwelcome flutter of attraction.

"That happens. I'm sure you're still tired from the trip up here. And, well, having a baby, I guess."

He sounded so considerate. His voice didn't hold the usual mocking tone she was so used to hearing. Her heart twisted as she thought of how their lives had diverged. At how his old appeal now morphed to attraction. At how he seemed to have become a different person.

"Sorry you had to get her," Erin mumbled, looking back down at Caitlin.

"It's okay. I didn't think she would settle for me."

"She's a good baby."

"Probably takes after her mom." His words were quiet, but they held a faint question in them. As if wondering if Caitlin's father had anything to do with her personality.

But Erin wasn't going down that road. She dragged one hand through the tangle of her hair, suddenly aware of how ragged she must look. Wearing the sloppy, comfy clothes she had put on last night after Dean left for the day. Her hair listing to starboard from the rough bun she had twisted her hair into.

An unwelcome memory of Kelly slipped into her mind. Trim. Slim and cute.

"So, are you going to be okay?" Dean asked.

"I'll be fine."

Suddenly she wanted him gone. She felt an unreasoning need to rush into the bathroom. Shower, clean up and put on decent clothes. Some makeup. Let him see her not as a disheveled mommy but an attractive woman. Why had she fallen asleep here?

She remembered working on her laptop. Putting together an ad proposal for a company. She glanced beside her, then the other side.

"What's the matter?" Dean asked.

"My laptop. I can't find it."

"Is this it?" Dean bent over and picked up her computer from the floor. But as he straightened he lost his balance. He shifted, tried to correct himself, but then fell sideways.

Against the table.

He cried out in pain and Erin jumped to her feet, still holding Caitlin. She caught him by the arm, much as he had done for her just a few moments ago, trying to pull him upright.

He was heavy, his arm like a band of steel under her hand. She didn't know if she would be able to get him balanced.

As soon as he regained his footing, he shook her arm off, his eyes narrowed, his jaw set in a hard line.

"I'm fine," he growled. "I didn't need your help."

She snatched her hand back, her head coming up, angry herself.

"Just doing for you what you did for me," she snapped, then she hitched her baggy pants up, drew Caitlin close and strode past him to the bathroom.

Dean knew he'd been a jerk just now. Erin was simply trying to help him just as he'd helped her. But it bugged him to look so helpless in front of her.

Dean watched her march away from him, with Caitlin in her arms. Frustration gripped him as he hobbled out of the room, thankful Erin wouldn't be able to see his painful and humiliating retreat. He wished he could have strided from the room as confidently as she had. Made a better exit than limping along like some old man, grabbing onto chairs as he rode out the burning agony in his leg.

He slowly came outside, then leaned against the house, giving himself some time to recover.

Cowboy up.

The cliché of rodeo riders everywhere echoed in his brain.

Well, he didn't know if he had to cowboy up. He wasn't a real cowboy anymore.

He heard the sound of a vehicle coming down the driveway so he stepped away from the house. He waited as Jan's truck, emblazoned with the sign "JP Construction," pulled up and stopped.

It was Jan and Leonard with the scaffolding. Dean made his way over, masking the throbbing in his leg. Wouldn't do for his boss to see how badly he was managing.

"Hey, thought we'd drop this off before we head over to Mercy," Jan said as he swung out of the cab. "Which side of the house do you want this on?"

"North side," Dean said. "It seems to be the worst so I was starting there."

"Sure thing." Jan got out, Leonard joining him. The young man wore his usual canvas bib overalls, his long hair anchored with a ball cap. Leonard was a good kid. Hard worker.

Dean shouldn't have been surprised that Jan was

taking him to work on the job at Mercy and leaving him here.

Leonard went to unload and Dean, knowing he couldn't do much to help them, hobbled back to where he was working to take the ladder down, gritting his teeth the entire time.

He cleaned up around the site while Jan and Leonard made quick work of setting up the scaffolding. He gathered up the debris he had created, bringing it to the pile he had started away from the house. Once he was done he could get Jan or one of his crew to help him haul it all away.

By the time he got back, the throbbing in his leg had thankfully settled to a dull ache. He looked up at the siding that had to be removed and the work that lay ahead, planning his week.

Is this really what you see yourself doing the rest of your life?

The thought created a flicker of panic. He had fallen into the carpentry work to fill time while his brother Vic was making plans with Keith McCauley. Plans put on hold when Lauren and Jodie had talked about selling the ranch.

But now that was settled and Vic was talking about expanding, making a place for Dean.

While part of him was excited at the thought, he couldn't ignore the fact that he hadn't been on a horse since the accident.

As he had said to his brother, what kind of rancher can't ride a horse?

But was carpentry really in his future?

"You got a lot done already," Jan said as he clambered down from the top of the scaffolding. "From the looks of it you'll be done this side by tomorrow."

His boss's simple compliment helped to assuage the feelings of uselessness swamping him.

"I think so."

"The windows will be coming in on Tuesday so we'll bring them Wednesday and help you install them." Jan rested his hands on his hips, looking the house over. "You figure the rest of the windows are okay?"

"They're a standard size so even if they did need replacing down the road we won't have to change the openings."

"This is a cool spot for a house," Leonard was saying as he joined Jan and Dean. "I think I could live here."

Dean had thought the same at one time. A memory of him and Tiffany walking around this house making dreams slipped through his thoughts, but as quickly as it came he dismissed it. She was history and while he had managed to forget her, her legacy still stuck with him. The look of pity on her face when she saw him lying in the hospital bed was one he'd never forget.

"It's a great house," he said. "Worth fixing up."

The door of the house opened and Dean felt an up-tick of his heart as Erin came around the side. Her hair was pulled up into a loose ponytail and she had changed into other baggy pants topped with a large sweater. Even in casual clothes and no makeup, she still looked amazing.

"Good morning, Jan," she said, avoiding Dean's gaze.

"Things are coming along well on your house," Jan

said, giving her a gentle smile. "Dean's doing a great job."

"I'm sure he is," Erin said, still not looking at him.

"I was just telling him we'll be putting the windows in on Wednesday. The forecast is for decent weather, but you might want to go to your sister's place with your baby that day. The house will get kind of chilly while we're working."

"Good to know. Thanks." She gave him a quick bob of her head. Then she turned to Leonard, holding her hand out. "Hi. I'm Erin."

"I'm Leonard. Dryden. Leonard Dryden that is."

Dean would have been blind not to notice the blush creeping up Leonard's neck, or the way he stared at Erin. Not that he blamed him, but he was surprised at how jealous he felt.

"Sorry. I should have introduced you," Jan said. "Leonard's family moved here a couple of years ago. He's been working for me since. Erin just moved here. She's Lauren McCauley's sister."

"I kind of figured," Leonard said, his hands resting on his hips, his head tilted to one side as if to examine her more closely. "You look exactly like her."

"She should," Dean put in. "They're twins." He wanted to blame the faintly acerbic tone in his voice on the fact that Leonard was the one chosen to work on the job in Mercy.

Instead of the fact that he was more annoyed at the way Leonard was looking at Erin.

"Really? You're that old?" Leonard's shock and the way he pulled his head back expressed his total disbelief.

"Thanks, I think," Erin said with a light smile.

"I mean, you look really pretty and all, but Lauren seems way older than you."

"Again, thanks." Erin's smile had deepened, softening her features, lighting up her eyes.

And the jealousy Dean felt in Leonard's presence only grew.

He had never been on the receiving end of a full-blown smile from Erin McCauley. The only smiles he got from her were either faintly mocking or faint, period.

"So, you single?" Leonard asked.

"Down, boy," Jan shot his helper a frown. "Let's talk about the windows. Unless you guys want to keep doing this?"

"No. Please let's talk about the windows." Erin turned back to Jan, remnants of her smile remaining.

"Like I said, I would recommend being gone that day," Jan said. "It's not supposed to be real warm and I don't think your baby would appreciate getting chilled."

"You got a baby? No way." Leonard's skeptical tone erased the last of Erin's humor. She nodded, slipping him a quick, sidelong glance.

"Yes. I have a little girl."

"Whoa. That's heavy duty."

He didn't actually take a step back, but Dean easily saw the retreat both in his expression and in his body language.

And it made him want to reprimand the kid. Especially when he saw the sorrow that clouded Erin's smile. He doubted she felt more than passing amusement initially, with Leonard and his puppy-dog admiration, but his sudden withdrawal must have been hard to take.

"She's really cute," Dean put in, feeling a need to defend her. "I even got to hold her this morning."

Finally Erin glanced his way, her expression holding a hint of thanks.

"How did you swing that?" Jan asked glancing from Erin to Dean, curiosity in his voice and eyes.

Dean wasn't sure how to answer that. Not without embarrassing Erin again.

"She even quieted down when I held her" was all he said, hoping the vague answer would keep more questions from Jan at bay.

Erin ducked her head and Dean guessed she was still embarrassed over what had happened this morning.

He felt bad that he had barged into the house, but hearing her baby crying for about ten minutes after he had arrived and not knowing how long she'd been before that, he'd figured he better check. Make sure nothing had happened to Erin. He hadn't seen her when he stepped into the house and had gone straight to Caitlin's room to find her squalling, her face red, her little hands bunched into fists, waving around.

He'd picked her up, bounced her, and had gone looking for Erin when she wasn't in the bedroom.

He'd found her lying on the couch and had panicked, thinking something had happened. He'd given her a shake while the baby slowly settled in his arms.

Thankfully she'd just been asleep. But the look of sheer terror on her face when she saw him holding Caitlin wasn't one he'd soon forget.

"Well, aren't you the fortunate one," Jan said, a meaning tone in his voice, his smirk telling Dean that he read the situation differently.

"I was just helping out," he protested, then caught himself from saying more.

"Of course you were," Jan said. "Which was why I knew you were the best man for this job."

Dean knew there were other factors at play, but he wasn't going there now.

"Anyhow, we should push on," Jan said, pulling his phone out of his pocket as it dinged and glancing at the screen. "And looks like I'm needed at the other site." He frowned, biting his lip, and Dean wondered what was going on.

Jan shoved the phone in his pocket and glanced from Erin to Dean. "So you'll be ready for the windows on Wednesday?" Jan asked.

"That should work." To get there would mean working tomorrow, a Saturday, but that didn't matter. Not like he had lots of other things going on in his life.

Jan waved goodbye and then they were walking back to the truck.

As soon as they drove away, Dean turned to get back to work. But was stopped by Erin's light touch on his arm.

"I never did say thanks," she said, her voice quiet, her eyes not meeting his. "For picking Caitlin up and settling her down this morning."

Dean wasn't sure what to say. If he were entirely honest with himself, that moment when Caitlin stopped crying, when her cries faded and she lay, for those few seconds pliant in his arms, he had felt a surprising tenderness.

And a flash of yearning.

"It was okay. I didn't mind," he said.

"I felt bad that I seemed abrupt with you."

He released a humorless laugh. "If anyone was abrupt it was me with you. I shouldn't have been such a jerk when I stumbled. You were just trying to help."

"I'm sorry—"

"No. Don't apologize for that. I'm the one that's sorry."

Their words hung between them. Two people trying to find their way through this awkward moment.

"Anyhow, thanks for getting Caitlin. That was really sweet of you." Erin peeked up at him through some loose strands of hair that had fallen away from her ponytail.

He had an unreasoning desire to reach out and tuck those strands behind her ear.

"You're welcome," he said, giving her a careful smile.

Their eyes held and in spite of everything Dean's heart rate jacked up. So did his breathing. Her lips parted like she was about to say something and the urge to curl her hair behind her ear was replaced by the urge to kiss her.

He shook the feeling off and turned away from her before he gave in to the impulse.

In another time and in another place he might have tried.

But he wasn't that guy anymore.

And she was never that girl.

Chapter Six

And so, Erin, I need to say that I'm sorry. I wasn't the father I should have been. I wish I could do it over, but I can't. In my own way I loved you. Please, remember that at least.

Erin finished the letter from her father and laid it down, sorrow threading through her as she looked around the ranch house that had been her childhood home.

When her sisters called yesterday morning, asking if she wanted to come to the ranch on Saturday for some sister bonding time, she had readily agreed. Dean was coming to work on the house again and for some reason, she wasn't sure she wanted to see him.

So she had come here yesterday. The three of them had taken Caitlin for a long walk around the ranch, had laughed, cried and shared stories, catching up on each other's lives. When Erin made a move to go home Jodie and Lauren had demurred, stating that Lauren had found a secondhand crib and put it in one of the rooms downstairs and fixed up her old room for her to sleep in.

She had agreed, but last night as she lay in her old bed in her old room, she had felt the same sorrow and regret her father now talked about in his letter. Her father's words resonated through her, bringing up memories and emotions.

While her sisters had resented their time here, she'd loved it. And guessed her father sensed that, too. They would talk about the ranch together, the few times they connected face-to-face. Sometimes she rode with him to move the cows.

Though he was a taciturn man, there was the occasional time he had told her she was a good girl.

For her father, that was high praise.

She looked down at the letter again, re-reading her father's apologies and struggled once again with a sense of shame. She certainly wasn't the innocent girl he was writing to and she wondered what he would think of her now.

And behind that, why she hadn't come more often to visit? She had all kinds of excuses for staying away and now, after reading her father's much-belated expressions of regret, they seemed facile. Lame.

She felt she should pray and ask God for forgiveness.

But she shook the feeling off. The same contrition that kept her from praying had kept her from attending church with her sisters this morning.

Then, before she could delve too deeply into her dark thoughts, the door of the ranch house burst open and Jodie and Lauren's laughter filled the eerie silence.

She got up from the couch, still holding Caitlin, and walked toward the porch just as her sisters came around the corner.

"Hey, you," Jodie said. "How was your morning?"

She gave her sister a quick hug, then stroked Caitlin's cheek with one finger. "And how's our baby girl?"

"We're both fine," Erin said. "How was church?"

"Pastor Dykstra had a good sermon and the music was great. Too bad you couldn't come."

Wouldn't come was more like it, but Erin wasn't about to admit that.

There was no way she, who once was such a strong proponent of morals and standards, could show up with a baby in her arms and no man at her side. Besides, she and God hadn't spent much time together the past while. It would seem hypocritical.

"Can you give me my niece?" Jodie asked, holding her hands out to her sister. "I need my Caitlin fix." Erin grinned as she carefully transferred Caitlin, still bundled up in a pink muslin blanket, to her sister. Caitlin's head twisted back and forth, her mouth opened and then she sank back into the sleep that had claimed her ever since Erin had fed her this morning. Jodie nuzzled her as she walked over to the couch.

"Did Aunt Laura play piano during the church service?" she asked Lauren as the latter plugged the kettle in, then came over and gave Erin a quick hug.

"No. They've got a new singing group at church. Jodie plays with them once in a while." Lauren's hand rested on Erin's shoulder as she held her gaze. "Did you have a chance to read your letter from Dad? What did you think?"

Erin wasn't sure how to articulate her emotions. "It was good to hear he regretted some of the things he did."

"Dad mellowed a lot before he died." Jodie looked

up from nuzzling Caitlin's cheeks. "He even apologized to me. For everything."

"I'm glad for you," Erin said.

Jodie and her father had had a complicated relationship. Jodie bore the brunt of his occasional bad moods the summers they'd spent with him after their mother died. Lauren and their father had a more practical, though distant, relationship. For some reason he and Erin got along. Mostly, she suspected, because she always did as she was told.

Caitlin started fussing and Erin took her from Jodie. "I think she needs to be changed. She fell asleep after I fed her last."

She snagged her diaper bag and walked through the kitchen, past her father's office to the bathroom at the end of the hallway.

Erin took the changing pad from her diaper bag, laid it down on the counter and laid Caitlin on it, smiling as her daughter's little hands batted the air. Her tiny mouth was pursed and her eyes were fixed on the light above the sink. Erin made quick work of removing the wet diaper.

While she worked she could hear the low murmur of her sisters talking and then heard her name mentioned.

"—just wish she could spend more time on herself," she heard Lauren say. "It's like she let herself go."

Erin stopped dead in her tracks at her sister's words, glancing down at the yoga pants and loose T-shirt she wore.

"Cut her some slack," Jodie protested. "She's a mom and probably dressing for comfort more than looks."

But while she guessed Jodie was sticking up for her, the comment made Erin feel worse.

She pulled back, returning to the bathroom to give her sisters a chance to finish their conversation.

But that was a mistake because when she stepped back in she caught her reflection in the mirror. No makeup, hair slightly askew from where Caitlin had grabbed it while she was burping her. The T-shirt was an older one and, at one time, she thought it attractive. It had an asymmetrical style with ruching caught by large wooden buttons down the side.

But now, with her sisters' words in her ears, she saw the missing button, the stain that never washed out. She saw the loose pants with their drawstring waist.

Is this what Dean saw?

She felt a shiver of revulsion, her mind racing back to the memory of Kelly and her snug jeans, cute T-shirt and perfect hair and makeup.

Erin knew it shouldn't matter what she looked like, but that her own sisters would mention it made her wonder what Dean saw when he glanced her way.

And why do you care?

She wasn't sure why. But she did.

Monday afternoon Erin parked her car in front of Brooke Dillon's hair salon, Cut and Run, and bit her lip.

"What do you think, baby girl?" she asked Caitlin, who was tucked away in her car seat in the back. "Am I being vain?"

Lauren's words from Sunday still echoed in her brain and while she knew she was taking them too much to heart, they still bothered her. This morning when Dean had arrived she waited until she knew he was working, then slipped out for her walk feeling suddenly self-conscious. And then she'd decided to go to town. Get her hair done.

But now that she was actually here, second thoughts assailed her.

Who are you trying to impress?

And as that last question slouched into her mind it was followed by a picture of Dean.

She pushed the car door open and got out, burying her changing feelings. It was just a cut and color. Something she'd needed for a while. Besides, it would be a great pick-me-up. A symbol of her new start here in Saddlebank.

As she stepped into the hair salon, Caitlin's car seat hooked on her arm the aroma of expensive shampoo blended with the pungent scent of hair dye and hair spray washed over her. Their Aunt Laura had taken them here once in a while to get their hair done and the smells brought back happier times in her life.

A woman with purple-and-pink-streaked hair looked up from the chest-high reception desk, the ring in her lip bobbing as she gave Erin a welcoming smile. "Welcome to Cut and Run. What can we do for you today?"

"I'd like a color and cut." She glanced around the full salon and realized how foolish her request was. Every chair was full and a few ladies sat in the reception area flipping through magazines.

The girl tapped her fingers on her cheek as she looked at the book. "I'm not sure we can get you in. Let me talk to Brooke." She left, and as the women with the magazines glanced her way, then at Caitlin, she felt a sudden need to retreat. One of the women was Kelly's mother. The other Erin recognized as one of the youth group leaders she had worked with a couple of summers all those years ago.

She was just about to turn to leave when someone called her name.

"Erin?"

Then Brooke herself came around the desk toward her. She wore a black silk blouse and a black skirt. Her blond hair was pulled back in an artful swirl of curls held by a glittering clip, and delicate silver chains hung from her ears. She looked elegant and beautiful and Erin felt even dowdier. The Brooke she remembered from her visits to Saddlebank had been less put-together. More casual. Looks like the roles were reversed now.

"I heard you were back in town," Brooke said, smiling at her. "Keira told me at church yesterday."

Of course. Erin should have known how quickly word got around a place like Saddlebank.

"How is Keira?" Erin asked.

"Great. She and Tanner are married. They have a little boy."

"Oh, that's great." Erin and Keira and Lauren used to hang out the summers they were back in Saddlebank. And though they had lost touch, she did know that Keira and Tanner had been dating and then broke up. She never knew the reason why. So she was glad to hear they were together again.

"And this must be Caitlin." Brooke leaned closer, her features softening as she touched Caitlin's cheek. "She's so precious." Brooke smiled, but then her smile seemed to shift and to hold a touch of sympathy as she straightened. "Your sisters seem crazy about her and I can see why."

Erin just nodded, far too aware of her washed-out shirt and loose-fitting blue jeans she thought would be suitable for a trip to town.

"I heard you wanted a color and cut?" Brooke asked, suddenly all business.

"It's okay. I can see you're too busy. I'll come back," she said, taking a step back to the door, her escape route.

Brooke waved off her objections. "Nonsense. I have time. Just come with me."

Miss Purple and Pink Hair frowned at her. "But I thought—"

"I have time," Brooke said, her voice firm. "Call Heather and reschedule. I know she won't mind."

"I don't want to cause any trouble," Erin objected. "Like I said, I can come back."

But Brooke was already walking away from her and the receptionist was already phoning so she followed along.

"So, your little girl going to be okay while we work?" Brooke asked as she pulled a cape off the chair and motioned for Erin to sit down.

"She's been fed and changed—"

"Oh, look at the adorable baby." An older woman who was sitting at one of the hair dryers flanking the wall got up and scurried over, her hair tucked into various bits of foil, a cape covering her clothes. She crouched down in front of the car seat, her hand stroking Caitlin's cheek. Then she looked up and Erin recognized Paige Argall, the town's librarian. "Hello, Erin," she said, her smile deepening as she got up. Then she gave Erin a quick hug. She pulled back, her hands on Erin's shoulders. "Welcome back to Saddlebank."

The warmth in her tone created a thickening in Erin's throat.

"Thanks."

"Is my niece here?" A voice called out and then Aunt Laura bustled into the salon. Short, plump, her graying hair cut in a shoulder length bob, Aunt Laura, with her smiles and good humor, was the exact opposite of her brother, Keith McCauley, Erin's father.

She hadn't had a chance to see her aunt yet and when Aunt Laura's arms slipped around her and pulled her close the tears that threatened came again. Erin let them flow for only a moment, then struggled to pull herself together.

"Oh, honey," Aunt Laura said, bracketing Erin's face with her plump, work-roughened hands. "What a long road you've been on to get back home."

Which just about set her off again.

"But have you seen her baby?" Mrs. Argall, still crouched down beside Caitlin, asked, unbuckling her. Then she looked up at Erin. "Can I take her out?"

"Only if you let me hold her, too," Aunt Laura insisted before Erin could say anything.

"We should get at the hair." Brooke pointed to the still empty chair and with a flush, Erin hurriedly sat down, hoping Caitlin would behave herself.

"You didn't need to cancel the other appointment."

"Heather won't mind," Brooke said.

"Oh, absolutely not," Paige added, cuddling Caitlin in her arms as she walked back to the dryer. "My daughter-in-law will do anything for a relative." Aunt Laura sat down beside her and they were joined by a young girl who was sweeping up.

"So what are we doing today?" Brooke asked as she fastened the cape around Erin's shoulders.

"I'm not sure exactly," Erin said, making a face at her reflection in the mirror. Her hair hung limp and boring around her face as Brooke pulled it free from the ponytail tie.

Brooke lifted and fluffed, angling her head this way and that, the diamond on her ring finger flashing in the lights from the salon. "We can go with lighter streaks on the top, darker on the bottom. To give the hair some definition. I wouldn't cut too much off, though."

Erin just nodded as Brooke made suggestions. She had no preference, only that something be done. She wanted a break from her past. A reason to feel better about herself.

Or so you can look good for Dean.

She pushed the thought aside, but it lingered as Brooke folded foils in her hair and painted color on them, bringing her up to date on all things Saddlebank. Erin found out that Heather was expecting, as was her sister-in-law Abby, who was married to Lee, Keira and Heather's brother. Allison Bamford, George Bamford's sister and Brooke's future sister-in-law, was going back to college. Alan Brady had expanded his mechanic business and an outsider had bought the grocery store.

But while she chatted, Erin gave her only half her attention. The other half was on Caitlin who was being cooed and oohed and aahed over by most everyone who was in the salon.

Seeing her daughter being passed around made Erin feel ashamed that she had stayed away from church, thinking people would judge her.

There hadn't been any condemnation in anyone's voice. No hint of reproach.

Only abundant acceptance and love.

And once again Erin had the feeling that moving back here had been the best thing she could have done for herself.

Dean carefully made his way down the scaffolding and when he got to the ground he stood back, a feeling of satisfaction washing over him. He had managed to finish off the siding as far down as he could reach.

And it looked great.

He heard the sound of a car arriving and he couldn't stop the silly lift of his heart.

Erin was home.

He wasn't going to go and check, but when her car door closed and he heard her walking to the house, he stopped piling up the scraps of siding he had dropped. Would she come and see what he'd done? Then the door of the house opened and his heart did that stupid jump again, but her footsteps returned to her car. This was repeated a few times until curiosity overcame his good sense.

When he came around the house, the hood of the trunk was up and all he could see of Erin was her feet.

"What's up?" he asked, hoping he sounded like he was simply making casual conversation. Not being snoopy.

Erin squealed her surprise, then slammed the trunk of the car shut.

And Dean could only stare.

Her hair was shinier, shorter and sort of sassy-looking. And she wore snug blue jeans and a pale pink, loose sweater over a white tank top. Gold hoops swung from her ears.

"Wow," he said, disappointed at how breathless the sight of her looking so different made him feel. "You look…amazing."

Her cheeks flushed and she ducked her head in a self-conscious gesture.

"I thought I should get something done to my hair and then I met up with Aunt Laura and we went shopping. I got some new clothes that I decided to wear right away."

"Well, you look great." Too late he realized how that might sound. "I mean, not that you didn't look great before."

"I looked like a college student cramming for finals," she said.

"You looked casual. Comfortable."

She grinned at that. "Thanks for that, but I think I like amazing better."

He wasn't sure what to say so he focused his attention on the boards of floor samples she had stacked against the car. "What are you planning?"

"I thought the inside of the house could use some work, too," she said, heaving the samples up by the handles. He hobbled over to help her, grabbing a couple of the samples, as well. These held various kinds of tile and the ones Erin carried to the house had pieces of wood attached to them.

"So what did you figure on doing?"

"I want to replace the flooring," she said as he tried to get ahead of her to open the door. But he couldn't keep up, his leg stiff from climbing up and down the scaffolding all day.

He was glad Erin hadn't been around to see his slow progress. It had been disheartening even though he had gotten more done than he figured.

If he didn't have his bad leg he would have been able to take down the scaffolding and accomplish so much more.

So now Erin was holding the door open for him and he had to move awkwardly past her, trying not to wince as he carried the heavy samples into the house.

"Just put them in the kitchen," she said as the door fell shut behind her.

"Where's Caitlin?" he asked as he carefully set the boards down, leaning them against the kitchen cabinets.

"Sleeping in her crib. She's had a busy day. Got passed around at Brooke's beauty salon while I got my hair done."

"I imagine she'd been quite the hit," he said with a grin. "She's such a little muffin."

Erin's expression grew suddenly serious and he wondered if he had overstepped some invisible line as she held his gaze. "I sure think so," she said, her voice quiet.

Dean wasn't sure what she meant by that or what he was supposed to say so he poked his chin toward the wood samples she was laying on the carpet of the living room. "I'm guessing you want to put down hardwood flooring?"

"And tile in the kitchen."

"That's a lot of work."

"I've done it before," she said casually. "In the house I owned in San Francisco."

"All by yourself?"

She chuckled at that as she stood up, walking around the samples as if surveying them from various angles. "No. I had help. Mostly my roommates and I, though Sam helped—" she stopped abruptly there.

Sam.

Dean remembered her saying that same name that morning when she had fallen asleep on the couch. She had sounded panicked when she said it, though.

"Was Sam one of your roommates?" he asked, trying to sound all casual. Like it didn't matter to him who this guy was.

Erin shook her head. "No. Just someone who helped out." Then she turned to him, her chin up, her eyes narrowing as they met his. "Actually, he's more than that. Sam is, no, was, Caitlin's father."

Dean heard the angry edge in her voice, the repressed anger.

"I take it he's not in the picture?" he asked, even though he knew he was edging toward a place he had no right to go.

"You take it correctly," she said, her shoulders lowering as she looked away. "He's not…not part of my little girl's life."

Which made him curiously relieved.

"Did you have any more samples to bring in?" he asked.

She shook her head. "No. But thanks so much for helping me."

"No problem."

He held her gaze a moment longer than necessary, as neither of them looked away. Old feelings blended with new and his breath caught in his chest.

Then Caitlin whimpered and his cell phone rang

and they broke the connection, each attending to other obligations.

And as Dean walked away, his phone still ringing, he felt a tiny sliver of hope because of her anger with Caitlin's father.

But even as he went through the usual list of "reasons why he couldn't date Erin," he couldn't discard the moments of connection he had felt around her. And this time around, he had a strong feeling she felt the same.

"Dean here," he said as he stepped out of the house, closing the door behind him.

"Yeah. Just thought I'd let you know that I can't come on Wednesday to help with the windows," Jan was saying. "Sorry about that. I can't come until Friday."

"Can you spare a guy to help me?"

"Not really. Sorry, bud. I'm running crazy here."

The apology puzzled him. "So, did you want me to come work on the Mercy job?"

"You could," he said after a long moment of silence. "I got all the guys I need but if you need to keep busy…" His sentence trailed off and while Dean appreciated the sentiment he also guessed that Jan was desperately thinking of a make-work project for him.

"That's okay," he put in, cutting off Jan's attempt to make him feel useful. "I've got enough here to keep me going for a while."

"You sure?"

"I'm sure. Thanks." He hung up and suppressed a sigh.

He knew that working for Jan was a two-way street. After his accident Dean had taken a couple of months off and Jan had held his job for him. As well, Jan had given him time off for his ongoing physiotherapy. Which he'd been neglecting the past months because he felt so guilty for having been away from the job so much.

Which meant he wasn't seeing the gains the physiotherapist promised.

He fought the usual feelings of uselessness, then pushed them aside. He'd just have to keep himself busy here. He really didn't have much choice.

He heard Erin talking quietly to Caitlin and he felt his own heart foolishly respond, thinking of that moment they'd shared.

He just hoped he'd be able to keep his wits about him around her.

Especially now that she was looking even better than before.

Chapter Seven

"So I thought you could ride Roany," Jodie said as she held the door of the house open for Erin, who carried Caitlin in her arms. They stepped outside and Erin couldn't stop a quiver of anticipation as they walked toward the corrals.

This morning Dean had come just for a short while and then left again. She had hoped to see him. To talk to him, but that chance was gone. She needed a distraction. So she'd called Jodie and asked if she could watch Caitlin. Asked if there was a suitable horse for her to ride. She wanted to go out into the hills she had spent so much time in as a young girl.

Thankfully Jodie had agreed. And she had her distraction.

All the way here her excitement had grown at the thought of going riding again. The sun was shining and the day was surprisingly warm for late September. "I thought you might not want to get too adventurous today so I picked my best-trained horse."

"No. I'd like to come back to Caitlin in one piece,"

Erin said with a chuckle, brushing a light kiss over her daughter's fuzzy head.

Though Erin had been excited about the prospect of spending some time alone, riding through the hills, the thought of leaving Caitlin behind also created a clench of uncertainty.

"You'll be okay, I'm sure of that," Jodie said as if sensing her second thoughts.

As they neared the corrals Erin saw a familiar truck parked there, as well. What was Dean doing here?

"Excellent. My helper has arrived," Jodie said.

"Helper?" Erin asked, puzzled why Jodie needed help with the horses.

"Yes. He's going to help me by going riding with you."

Was this why he had left early this morning?

Erin wasn't sure how to process this. Not sure she wanted to have Dean with her on what she had hoped to be a time of solitude.

And yet the thought held a surprising appeal.

"I wanted to make sure you'd be okay," Jodie said as they walked toward Dean. He was petting Mickey, one of their older horses who was also tied up.

"Hey, Dean," Jodie called out as they came closer. "Thanks for coming."

Dean straightened, but the brim of his cowboy hat shadowed his eyes. By the grim set of his mouth Erin guessed that he wasn't entirely pleased with the unfolding events.

"So, you want me to go riding with Erin?"

He didn't sound happy about it. At all. Did he know what he was in for?

"I need to know that Erin will come back in one

piece." Jodie's grin and perky tone showed Erin she wasn't the least bit fazed by Dean's apparent antagonism.

"I can go on my own." Erin wasn't sure she wanted to spend time with someone who clearly didn't want to be doing this.

Or didn't want to be with her.

"I'm sure you can, but you're a mom now and I'm your daughter's aunt and if something were to happen to you I would feel horrible. I'm sure Dean can agree with me there."

Dean didn't reply, instead he busied himself adjusting the saddle, checking the stirrups with jerky movements. To keep himself from looking at either of them, Erin guessed.

"Okay, then, maybe you two should get going," Jodie said, reaching out to take Caitlin from Erin.

Her trepidation returned with a vengeance at the sight of Dean avoiding her.

"I can do this another day," Erin protested.

"Today works best for you and for Dean," Jodie said, seemingly unfazed by the obvious reluctance of the two main participants. She kept her hands out and Erin reluctantly handed over her baby to her sister.

"Okay, then, I'll go," she said knowing that her sister could be more stubborn than her. If she gave in, she and Dean could go for a short ride, placate her sister and come back right away.

She drew in a deep breath, brushed her hands over her jeans, then walked over to Roany and slowly untied the leather reins.

Dean walked around his horse and did the same. She lifted her foot to the stirrup and with one little hop managed to get astride the horse. Roany didn't so much as blink.

"Stirrups okay?" Jodie asked while Erin tested their length, the leather of the saddle creaking as she did so.

She nodded, then glanced over at Dean, wondering why he was waiting. Was he changing his mind about coming along?

But while he stood by his horse, his hand on the pommel, reins gathered in his hands, shoulders rising and falling as he breathed she felt a sudden flash of insight.

How would he get on with his bad leg? She knew he was proud and she guessed that he didn't want them to watch.

"Actually, this one on the left is a bit wonky," she said, turning away from Dean, bending down to inspect a nonexistent problem on the opposite side of her horse.

Jodie looked confused and Erin shot her a warning look, tilting her head ever so slightly in Dean's direction, hoping her outspoken sister would play along.

Jodie seemed to get the hint, because she started to fuss with the stirrup with one hand while she rocked Caitlin in her other arm. "I think it's okay," she said. "Let me have another look."

While they fiddled and adjusted a buckle that was fine, Erin could feel the tension emanating from the man beside her. She shot her sister a meaningful look, hoping Jodie understood what she was telegraphing.

What were you thinking?

But Jodie just bent over enough to look under Erin's horse, then gave her sister a discreet thumbs-up. She guessed Dean was finally mounted.

"There we go. I guess Mommy's stirrup is all good to go," Jodie said to Caitlin, nuzzling her with the tip of her nose. Then she flashed Erin a grin as she stepped back. "Have fun. Do you have your cell phone?"

Erin nodded, patting the button-down pocket of her shirt just to make sure. "Caitlin should be good for the next couple of hours. I did put a bottle in her diaper bag if she gets fussy." But even as she spoke the words so confidently she felt a tremor of apprehension. What if Caitlin cried too hard? What if something happened to her? Was she being irresponsible by leaving like this? "You're sure you're going to be okay?" she asked again.

"We will be fine," Jodie assured her. "I'm looking forward to some aunty-and-niece time." She stepped away from the horse and tossed off a wave to Dean. "Thanks so much for going with my sister, Dean. I feel better knowing that she's with you."

Erin shot a quick sidelong glance at Dean. She couldn't see his eyes as his hat was pulled down low, but his jaw was clenched, his hands bunched on the reins. He looked like he was in a lot of pain, which puzzled her. Though she had never witnessed it, she knew he climbed up and down ladders and scaffolding at her house.

Maybe this was different for him?

Anger at Jodie flashed through her for pushing Dean to do this. But she kept her comments to herself. They would make this ride quick to keep up appearances. As soon as was reasonable, she would be coming back.

"If you're ready to go, we should leave," Dean said his voice sounding strained as he kept his gaze firmly on his horse's head.

She pulled gently back on the reins, shifting her

weight, signaling to Roany that she wanted to back up. And just like that her horse dropped his head and took a few hesitant steps back then stopped when Erin settled ahead again.

Like riding a bike, she thought, shooting another glance at her baby, tucked now in her sister's arms.

"You'll be okay?" she asked, trying not to sound like a harried mother, but feeling like a string that tied her to Caitlin was slowly being pulled tighter with each move away from her.

"We'll be fine," Jodie assured her.

Then there was nothing left to do but leave.

"Maybe just make a few turns around the yard at first," Dean suggested, pulling his reins to the side, turning his horse away from Jodie. "Just to get the horse used to you and you comfortable with the horse."

Erin simply nodded, doing as he said, putting Roany through a few turns, to the left, then to the right. The gelding easily responded to her lightest touch of the reins on his neck, the faintest nudge of her heels in his sides. "I think I'm good," she said, noticing, with surprise, that Dean did the same thing. Probably just getting used to an unfamiliar horse.

"You sure?"

"You know where to go?"

"I've ridden this ranch many times."

He sounded strained and she could see lines of tension around his mouth.

"Are you sure about going?" she asked. "We can do this another day."

"No. We're here now. May as well do this."

He sounded angry so Erin said nothing more, realizing that pushing the issue too hard would humiliate him. Oh, well. He had to know what he was capable of. So she followed him as he rode around the large red barn where a tractor and baler were parked. Just where her father always had it.

Erin felt the pull of nostalgia and a thread of sorrow at the sight. Her life had been so crazy the past while that she felt as if she hadn't even had time to mourn her father. To miss him. She thought again of the letter she had skimmed, vowing to read it more closely tonight.

Dean seemed to know where he was going so she was content to follow him past the yard and along the rail fence edging the winter pasture for the cows. A trail led from here into the trees and then up the hills toward a lookout point she rode to when she was younger.

Dean sat awkwardly in the saddle and Erin could see he was favoring his injured leg. Though she wanted to ask him if he wanted to quit she knew it would insult his pride. She'd seen a few flashes of that the past few days.

She watched him from behind as he slowly, imperceptibly seemed to relax. To sit back, his shoulders lowered, his hips centered, swaying gently with the horse.

The air was cooler in the shade of the trees, a whispering breeze scattering golden leaves on the path and on them. Soon the trees would be entirely orange and yellow, and the countdown to winter would begin. Erin couldn't help a touch of sentimentality. She and her sisters had never been here through the fall. They'd spent that time back in Knoxville and as soon as they were old enough, they'd stopped coming back to the ranch.

Had their father missed them? They never knew

because he never answered any of their letters or returned their phone calls.

How lonely it must have been for him here!

Erin shook off the gloomy thoughts, preferring to focus on this time here and now. To enjoy the silence, and, if she was honest with herself, some time with Dean away from the house.

They rode on, the thud of the horses' hooves the only other sound in the gentle quiet. And as they did, Erin felt peace slowly wash over her. Finally they came to a place where the trail widened out and Dean pulled back for her to catch up to him.

"You doing okay?" he asked, glancing down at her feet as if making sure the stirrups she and Jodie had been fussing with were good.

"I'm just fine," she said, giving him a cautious smile. She wanted to ask him the same, but if he wasn't he wouldn't say, and if he was she didn't need to ask.

But from the tightness around his mouth, she guessed it was a struggle for him.

They rode for a while and finally Erin couldn't stand it any longer. "Look, I'm sorry you got roped into this, if you'll pardon the cowboy reference. I didn't have anything to do with it. I just wanted to go riding, like I used to. I didn't ask if you could come along."

She shot him a concerned sidelong glance, but he kept his face resolutely ahead, as if he didn't want to look at her.

"I'm sure this was Jodie's idea," she continued. "You riding with me."

"Vic's, too," he said. "He called me at your house to tell me that Jodie needed some help. When I came here I found out this was what she wanted help with."

He kept his gaze fixed on the trail ahead, his eyes narrowed. She wanted him to look at her so she could read his expression better.

"I'm sorry this took you away from your work," she added. She guessed he was angry or in a lot of pain. What she wished he would do was either get over it or admit it and stop. She preferred not to keep riding if he was going to be all annoyed or if his injury would get worse.

He shrugged, shifting in the saddle again, his jaw clenching.

"Doesn't matter," he replied, his tone terse. "Truth is, I was done and my boss Jan didn't have any work for me on the job in Mercy. So it's not like I'm out anything because of this." He didn't sound pleased. They rode along for a while longer, but Erin was far too aware of the tension in the air. This wasn't how she had envisioned her ride so she pulled her horse to a stop.

"Look, again, I'm sorry you had to do this," she said, struggling to keep the frustration out of her voice at her repeated apologies. "We should just go back or you can go back on your own and I can keep riding."

He pulled up as well, his horse shaking his head at the sudden stop, bridle jangling. Dean just looked ahead, as if ignoring her, then finally he turned to face her.

"I'm sorry," he said finally, his voice sounding rough. "I know I'm being a jerk. I know I have been a jerk the last few days. It's just…" his voice trailed off and he winced, adjusting his seat and stretching out his one leg. Then he gave her an apologetic look. "This is the first time I've been on a horse since the accident."

Erin could only stare at him, surprise and shock flowing through her. "You mean…you're saying…"

"I'm saying I haven't ridden since I got out of the hospital."

"Because you can't?"

Dean pressed his lips together, looking ahead again. "No. My physiotherapist encouraged me to ride."

"Then why not?"

He said nothing for a moment, which made Erin even more curious.

"I haven't because…" He paused, as if the words were too hard to get out.

But Erin waited, sensing he was on the cusp of something difficult. Something important.

He moved to one side, wincing, then shook his head lightly, as if shaking off an errant thought.

He finally looked directly at her, his hat tipped back so she could see his eyes, the sheen of sweat on his face she hadn't noticed before.

"Because I'm afraid."

Chapter Eight

His words echoed in the silence. He had never dared admit that to anyone before. To say the words aloud, to talk openly about his fear made him feel foolish and weak. But when he looked at Erin the only thing he saw was admiration.

"Are you afraid now?" she asked.

Dean squeezed his hands to stop the trembling and looked ahead again, drawing in a long, slow breath. "Not as much as when I started."

It was pride pure and simple that got him to the ranch. When he'd found out what Jodie had wanted help with, his initial response was to outright refuse. Until she'd said she needed his help with Erin. His ego had taken a beating the past while with her and he couldn't stand for it anymore. When Jan had called to offer him the job in Mercy he knew he was only doing it out of sympathy.

And he was tired of it. Tired of looking like the helpless ex-cowboy. Out of anger and frustration he'd agreed.

Trouble was, he didn't know how hard it was going

to be once he faced the horse. But Erin was there and Jodie was watching. It had been pride that got him awkwardly in the saddle and stubbornness that kept him mounted.

Thankfully neither Jodie nor Erin had to witness his ungainly and fearful clamber onto the horse. And even more important, Mickey had stood solid as a rock while his good foot scrabbled to find the stirrup, his heart thudding like a jackhammer in his chest.

He had hoped to do a few more circuits around the yard to ease the pounding in his heart, but Erin seemed to catch on very quickly. So he simply had to push on and hope the fear would die down. That and the pain that was like shards of glass in a leg unaccustomed to this position.

"So you haven't ridden at all before this?"

"No. I tried to mount up a couple of times but just couldn't make that final move."

"Do you want to get off now? Rest for a few minutes? I'd like to check out Pigeon Point."

"Pigeon Point? I've never heard it called that before."

"My dad took us here once. To shoot clay pigeons."

In spite of the pain shooting through his knee and the fear that still hovered, Dean had to smile. "Can't imagine that."

"I have a country side," she returned. "So, you game?"

Dean nodded, but then realized if he got off, he would have to find a way to get back on again. Or run the risk of leading his horse all the way back to the ranch.

He was about to change his mind but Erin had already dismounted and was leading her horse to a nearby tree. So he slowly pulled his foot out of the stirrup, then rolled himself sideways and slid off the saddle, landing on his good leg, flinching when Mickey moved his feet as if impatient.

But nothing happened and his racing heart rate eased down again.

He stretched and tested his weight, thankful the pain was ebbing away. He was pleased it didn't hurt more. Maybe his physiotherapist was right. He needed to ride again.

He led Mickey to a tree close to Roany and quickly tied him off.

Erin had pulled her cell phone out of her pocket and thumbed it on.

"Calling to check in?" he asked, a playful note in his voice.

"Yes, I am," she said sounding somewhat defensive. "This is the first time I've been away from Caitlin and I know Jodie is my sister, but still—"

"I get it," Dean said, flashing her an understanding smile. "I was just teasing you."

Her mouth twitched, but she completed the call anyway. From what she was saying to her sister it sounded like all was well with her daughter. He walked away to give her some privacy.

A worn path led through an opening in the trees. He knew about this lookout point. Had ridden past it many times on his way to the far pasture to check on the cows. He'd never had the time to stop and look, but judging from the easily visible path, other people had.

He pushed through the underbrush and the land opened up and flowed away from him. The Saddlebank River spooled out below him a band of silver, flashing in the sun, flanked by clusters of trees that showed hints of the orange and yellow that would soon blaze from this valley.

He heard a rustling behind him and there was Erin, her hands shoved in the back pockets of her jeans, a smile playing over her face as she looked out over the valley.

"I forgot how beautiful it is here," she said, a reverent tone in her voice. Then she eased out a sigh, lowering herself to the ground. "Do you mind if we sit awhile? If we're going to be admitting stuff, my legs are sore, too." She flashed him a smile, her hair bouncing on her shoulders, her eyes fringed with dark lashes drawing him in.

"I don't mind." Spending time with Erin held a bittersweet appeal. But as he clumsily sat down he was reminded again of his own weakness.

She pulled her legs up, wrapping her arms around them, then glanced his way again. "I feel like I have to apologize yet again for my sister's unwelcome intervention. I don't think she realized—"

"That this ex–saddle bronc rider is afraid of horses?" He couldn't keep the bitter tone out of his voice. "Wait until that gets out."

She ducked her head and looked away and once again he felt like a heel for being so abrupt. He wanted to blame the throbbing in his leg, though it was easing away, or the relief he felt now that he'd survived his first time back on a horse. But there was more. A feeling of not knowing who he was anymore.

"I don't think anyone would have guessed that," she said, her voice quiet. "And I won't say anything if you don't." Then she gave him a careful, sidelong glance and he recognized her gentle peace offering. A way of bridging a gap he had created.

"It's just… I've wanted to be a saddle bronc rider as long as I could ride. I lived for the thrill, the challenge, the pitting of my skills against this out-of-control animal." He leaned back against the tree behind him and stretched out his leg. "Sounds kind of shallow, but it was my life. Who I was."

"I remember watching you that one summer," she said, resting her chin on her knees as she looked out over the valley. "I thought you were good."

Her praise warmed him more than it should.

"I never knew. I always got the impression that what I did was beneath you. That going to rodeos was for rednecks and cowboys."

"You can't live in Saddlebank and not go to the rodeo at least once," she said with a grin. "My sisters convinced me I should go. You were competing that night and, well, I was impressed."

"Really? I impressed you?" he asked.

"If you're fishing for compliments, you already got one bite." She shot him a sideways glance. Added a smile. Tucked her hair behind her ear.

The tilt of her head, the glint in her eye, the half smile made him wonder if she was flirting with him.

"So you must miss it?" she asked, her voice growing more serious.

"I do." The simple statement didn't cover the disappointment twisting his stomach at the idea that he couldn't do the one thing that he thought defined him. "It was who I was. What I wanted to be. Everything I ever did was with the hope of competing at a higher level."

"And the lifestyle? Do you miss that, too?"

Her question puzzled him. "What do you mean?"

She shrugged. "Sorry. None of my business."

He looked over at her, but her eyes were fixed on the valley below them. Yet something about the question she asked niggled other thoughts. Questions he'd had himself the past half year. Before his injury he'd been on the road more and more. Gone from the ranch. Riding over the weekends. Partying hard with his buddies.

His accident, however, had shifted his point of view. And thinking about his previous life, sitting beside the one person he'd always considered the epitome of goodness and kindness, pushed him even further down the path he'd started in the hospital room. When the doctor told him how long rehabilitation would take.

"Truth to tell, I don't miss the overall lifestyle," he said. "And looking back now, I knew how shallow it was. Lying in a hospital bed for an extended period tends to give a guy some perspective. I had time on my hands. And one of the things I thought about was something you said to me the last time I saw you. That summer you spent here in Saddlebank."

She shot him a look of puzzlement. "What was that?"

"That I was headed down a one-way road to nowhere. That the journey would make me unhappy and unsatisfied." He lifted his knee, resting his forearm on it as he fiddled with a piece of grass. "I think getting injured was a reality check and a chance to reassess my life. My girlfriend had broken up with me and for a while I blamed her. I blamed Vic. I blamed everyone. But then I thought of what you said and I got to look back over my life through your eyes. And I didn't like what I saw."

"Why are you telling me this?" she asked, looking ahead. He wasn't sure how to read her expression.

"Because I know what you thought of me then." Dean knew he was exposing his deeper self. Things he'd hidden all these years under a blanket of swagger and tough talk. But she'd already seen him at his most vulnerable. Had heard about his fear and seen his helplessness. It bugged him and he hated admitting that, but he wanted her to know her opinion had mattered.

"I know I wasn't good enough for you. You weren't the only one who thought that. You were this sweet, caring person who was a strong Christian. I know I poked fun of that part of your life and I'm sorry." He stopped, feeling again the shame that had dogged him the past few months since the time he'd begun reading his Bible again. Returning to the faith he had once mocked. He had his ups and downs and his moments of weakness, but he felt he was taking slow, uncertain steps back to his faith. "In spite of how I acted and how I treated you I think there was always a part of me that wanted to be worthy of you. I never really forgot you."

There. It was out. Poor, lonely Dean. Always keeping a space in his heart for a girl who had never encouraged or shown him that he mattered to her as much as she had mattered to him.

"You should have" was all she said. "You should have put me right out of your head."

She blinked and he was shocked to see a tear trickling down the side of her face. She quickly swiped it away, but it was too late.

"What's wrong?" He moved closer, and gave in to

the impulse he had felt previously and gently brushed her hair back from her face. "I'm sorry if something I said bothered you."

She had gone perfectly still and he thought he had gone too far, intruding too closely into her personal space.

But as her eyes met his a feeling of rightness permeated the atmosphere. That everything he had waited for and wanted at one time was right here. His breath quickened and he felt as if the world had narrowed down to this moment, this space. Just the two of them.

He let his finger trail down her cheek, easing away the tears that had drifted down.

"You're so beautiful," he whispered, the words slipping past old barriers that didn't seem as necessary as they once were. "You always were."

"Why…why did you always ask me out?"

Her unexpected question set him back, but he recognized her attempt to bridge the then and now.

Well, he had started this. May as well take the full plunge into humility.

"Like I said, even though I was a jerk, a part of me always appreciated your faith. I know many of the girls I dated weren't the kind of girl I would bring to see my mom. But you were. You had a sweetness that intrigued me. A goodness that, whether I wanted to admit it or not, was something I wanted in my life. I just thought I was too cool to try. But you…" He paused, cupping her face in his hand, his thumb caressing her chin, surprised that she allowed him to do this. "You were special. Pure."

Even as he spoke the words he realized how they

might sound to her, given that she had come to Saddle-bank with a baby. Yet, he still meant them.

Her eyes locked on his, and her hand came up and gently covered his, pressing his hand against her face.

He stopped breathing for a moment, connected by the warmth of her palm and his hand on her face.

"Erin," he said softly, leaning in, trying to get closer to her.

She didn't look away and all the intervening years fell away as he closed the distance between them. As his lips brushed hers he felt as if he was finally where he should be.

Her breath sighed against his mouth. Then her other hand came up and cupped his cheek, and when he gently pulled away they stayed connected. Hands. Eyes. Hearts.

"You are such an amazing person," he said, holding her gaze, wanting to extend the moment, to build on the connection they had just shared. "I've always admired you. Always appreciated who you were. You made me…made me want to be a better person."

Her expression hardened and the words he thought might encourage her made her pull back.

Then she released a harsh laugh, pulling back from him and breaking the connection.

"You don't know anything about me anymore," she said. "I'm not that same girl now."

"You may not think so, but I know you're the same caring, loving person. The same faithful Christian."

She just looked at him. "I'm a single mother."

He heard the unspoken hurt in the words and guessed how she saw herself. "You have a little girl," he said. "But to me that doesn't change anything."

"I haven't been in church for months."

"I didn't think I belonged there, but church has become a place I feel like my soul can rest when I'm there. I feel like I get support and strength to carry on for the week." He was quiet, realizing the irony of the situation. Him encouraging her to go to church when years ago it would have been the other way around. "Why don't you come on Sunday?"

She looked away from him, her eyes resting on some faraway place across the valley as if looking back over her life. "I don't know. It will be hard."

"I'll be there."

He threw the words out casually hoping they would encourage her.

She gave him a weary look, then shook her head as if pushing the thought aside and quickly got to her feet, ending the conversation. "I think we should go back to the ranch."

Then before he could say anything, she turned and strode away from him, scattering leaves as she plunged into the underbrush.

Dean dragged his hands over his face. This wasn't the first time she'd pushed him away. But it was the first time he'd kissed her.

He rolled onto his good knee and slowly got up, grabbing a nearby tree branch to stabilize himself. He caught his balance, his leg stiff and sore, frustration clawing at him once again. Had he misread her so badly?

For a brief moment after he kissed her, he'd thought things were changing between them. But as he limped to where the horses were tied he realized he faced another dilemma. How to mount the horse with legs that still felt the strain of riding. He paused, watching Erin easily mount up.

Please, Lord, he prayed as he walked over to his horse. *Let me get on the horse in one go.*

After spilling his guts to her and having her push him away—again—he figured he could use a win.

Erin rode back to the ranch, her mind a whirl of emotions.

What had she done? Why had she let Dean kiss her? She didn't have room in her messy life for this. She wished she could put it behind her, but her heart was still trembling from the feel of his mouth on hers.

Even now she was too aware of Dean behind her as they rode back to the ranch. How would she cope with him at her house every day after this?

Roany whinnied as they came closer to the ranch and as they came around the barn she saw Jodie walking toward the house.

What was she doing? Did she leave Caitlin alone in the house?

But as her sister turned, Erin saw her holding her daughter, and her fear eased.

Too vulnerable, she thought as her heart slowed again. Too many things happening too quickly. And the man behind her was part of her fragile and teetering emotions.

Jodie walked toward them, and as she came nearer Erin caught her frown. "I thought you guys would be gone much longer," Jodie called out.

"I got sore," Erin said. It wasn't entirely untrue, though any stiffness she'd felt after not being in the saddle for so long had eased away by the time they came back to the ranch.

"I figured you were being too ambitious taking on such a long ride."

"Bit off more than I could chew," Erin muttered as she slowly dismounted. She loosened the halter rope off the saddle horn and tied Roany to the hitching rail, dismayed to see her hands still trembling.

"Did you at least have fun?"

Erin chose to ignore the insinuation in her sister's voice, baffled once again at the shift in Jodie's attitude toward Dean.

Which, in turn, only proved to show her how completely the axis of her life had tilted.

"Yeah, it was good" was all she said, keeping any emotion out of her voice.

She caught Jodie's puzzled look but ignored her, slipping the reins over Roany's head and letting him spit out the bit.

"How are you feeling, Dean?" Jodie called out, looking past Erin to where she guessed Dean was slowly dismounting.

Erin tried not to pay attention to him, just as she had back in the clearing when he'd struggled to get back on his horse. Though she hadn't looked directly at him it had been painful to witness what she had. At one time Dean could easily vault on a horse in one smooth movement and had, the few occasions she'd seen him, done so with a flourish and a cocky tip of his hat to her.

But this Dean was awkward and ungainly and she guessed, ashamed of his disability. As a consequence the ride back to the ranch had been quiet. And the entire time Erin had stayed ahead of Dean, struggling with her changing emotions.

They were having such a nice visit until he'd brought up the past. The other Erin.

There was always a part of me that wanted to be worthy of you.

She knew he meant the words as an encouragement and at one time they might have been. But now, after the past year of her life, they felt more like a condemnation. She who had prided herself on her values, her faith, had helped a married man break his promises.

"I'm okay. I'll be stiff this afternoon," Dean said with a grunt as he slipped the saddle off Mickey.

Erin finally got her own saddle off and set it on its edge by the fence. Dean was already leading his horse to the pasture. He favored his good leg more than ever and again Erin looked away, quite sure he didn't want spectators.

Then Caitlin let go a little peep, lifting her head from Jodie's shoulder, then dropping it again.

"Can you take Roany back to the pasture?" Erin asked, handing the reins to her sister. "I'll take Caitlin."

Jodie did as she was asked, shifting Caitlin to Erin's arms and taking the reins.

Erin held her daughter close, brushing a gentle kiss over her head, inhaling the sweet, precious scent of her as she hurried back to the house. She probably should thank Dean for coming with her on the ride, but she wasn't the one who had asked him so she figured Jodie could do the honors.

She just wanted to retreat, to create some space between Dean's words and her present reality. But as she stepped into the house, she realized her mistake.

Memories of her father's letter bombarded her as she walked into the living room. She had sat exactly here while she read the letter that stated the same things Dean had just told her. What a good, sweet girl she was and how sorry he was that he didn't take care of her or appreciate her like he should have.

If she was a more philosophical person she might think her relationship with Sam was a way of dealing with her "daddy" issues. But the reality was simpler. She thought she loved him and he would give her the happily-ever-after she had always envisioned. A husband. A home. And someday, a family.

First comes love, then comes marriage, then comes Erin with a baby carriage.

But she'd got that wrong, too.

She looked down at her daughter, a motherly rush of love washing over her.

"I promise to take care of you," she whispered.

And even as she spoke her errant thoughts drifted back to Dean and the kiss they'd shared. The changing of the relationship she didn't dare indulge in.

She put Caitlin in her bouncy chair, then hurried to wash her hands. But through the window above the sink she could look over the yard.

Jodie and Dean were talking while he brushed down the horses. She saw Jodie's hands fluttering the way they always did when she was fired up about something. Erin wondered what it could be.

She settled on the couch, watching Caitlin, who was batting her tiny hands at the animals suspended above the bouncy chair. She had already grown so much and was becoming more aware of her surroundings. And each change made Erin realize how much her baby depended on her to make a home and a place.

Erin leaned forward to adjust her blanket around her legs and as she did she saw a Bible sitting on the table. Jodie's? Lauren's? Did it matter?

One of her sisters was nourishing her soul.

Erin had moved away from her God the past year. Sam wasn't a Christian and though he had never mocked her faith, he had never encouraged it, either.

And why would he? That would mean coming face-to-face with what he was doing to his family.

She pulled the Bible closer and opened it to one of the bookmarked pages.

Her eyes skimmed over the verses, then stopped at one that was underlined.

"Psalm 146:9. *The Lord watches over the foreigner and sustains the widow and the fatherless.*"

The passage struck a chord deep in her lonely soul.

Her daughter was fatherless and it hurt Erin more than she could say. She had grown up in a broken family and she wanted more than the mess that was her childhood for any child she would have.

Erin put the Bible down and pressed her fingers to her eyes, other memories intruding on her fragile peace. During the last few months of their relationship things hadn't been going well for her and Sam. She had talked about ending it. But Sam had broken down, pleading with her to stay with him. In a moment of weakness and possibly fear of being alone, Erin had given in.

It was that night Caitlin was conceived.

And it was a week later that Sam's wife, Helen, holding their five-year-old daughter, stood on her doorstep, begging her to let Sam go. To stop seeing him.

That was the first she'd known of Sam's marriage and his unfaithfulness to his wife. She'd broken up with him immediately.

Five weeks later she found out she was pregnant.

Erin fought down the memories, wishing she could find some peace from the guilt and shame that haunted her still. She was tired of crying over things she couldn't control and the breakdown of a marriage she knew nothing about.

Yet she felt responsible.

Therefore, there is now no condemnation for those who are in Christ Jesus.

The Bible verse from Romans that she had at one time memorized shimmered on the edges of her mind like a promise. But somehow she couldn't make it real or make it her own.

Then the door opened and her sister swept in, scattering her self-recrimination.

"Has Dean left?" she asked, quickly setting the Bible aside.

"Yes. Did you want him to stay?"

Erin waved off her question. "Just curious, that's all."

"So, did you enjoy yourself?" Jodie asked, lowering herself to the floor beside her niece. She stroked Caitlin's cheek and was rewarded with a lopsided smile. "Look, she's smiling at me."

"It's just gas," Erin returned.

"You say gas, I say smile." Jodie seemed unfazed by Erin's semigrouchy reply as she lifted Caitlin out of the chair. "And you love your Aunty Jodie, don't you," she said, switching to the singsongy tone women everywhere use with babies. "You been giving Aunty Jodie smiles all morning though it was a lot shorter morning than I thought it would be. Mommy says she got stiff and sore, but I think something else was going on, don't you?"

Erin chose to ignore her sister's not-so-subtle subtext. "I should probably head home, too."

"To what?" Jodie gave her a pointed look.

"I need to get some work done before I order flooring. I'm thinking of redoing the kitchen. Putting tile down there and hardwood in the living room."

But Jodie would not be deflected. "Dean seemed in a rush to leave."

Erin guessed her sister was fishing, but Erin wasn't biting.

"Did you have a fight with him?" Jodie pressed. "Did he come on to you again?"

Erin thought of that moment when his hand had cupped her chin. That electric moment when they had kissed.

"He did, didn't he?"

"You wouldn't have sounded so happy about that a few years ago." Erin knew the blush warming her cheeks only affirmed what her sister said, so she didn't bother refuting the comment.

"I know. But people change," Jodie said. "He comes to church now and I know it means something to him."

And didn't that only add to her own burdens? "I've changed a lot the past few years, too."

Jodie looked down at Caitlin, the clear evidence of that change.

"How much different are you from when you were younger. The dear, sweet sister we've always loved?"

"Enough to have a baby."

Jodie snorted. "Seriously, do you think you're the only female in the history of women who ended up in this situation?"

"It's not that simple."

"Actually, it's fairly simple."

Erin wanted to challenge her statement, but if she did, too much would come out. Things she wasn't ready to face herself.

Jodie held her gaze for a few more beats, then nodded, as if acknowledging that this topic was closed.

"So we'll talk about something else. I was wondering if you would be willing to come with me to Bozeman next week. I thought you and Lauren could try on bridesmaid dresses."

"Of course. I have some time between jobs."

"What are you doing now?"

"Book cover mock-ups for a publishing company I hope to get work with and an advertising campaign that isn't due for a month yet."

"You've kept busy with your work?"

"Not as busy as I want to be." She could use some more of it. Like she'd told her sisters, she had a few feelers out, but nothing substantial had come back yet.

From there the conversation slipped to Jodie's job, Lauren working at the flower shop and the plans for Jodie's wedding.

But even as they talked, she couldn't help the tiny flicker of unwelcome jealousy at how settled Jodie's and Lauren's lives had become. Future husbands, a home they would be sharing. She tried not to let panic come over her as she looked at Caitlin, so helpless and so dependent as she lay quiet in Jodie's arms. The fact that she was solely responsible for her daughter's upbringing became more real the more time she spent here.

But you're not on your own.

She looked at her sister and though she knew that was true, she still felt left behind. Alone.

You don't have to be.

And why did those words bring up a picture of Dean? Holding her chin, looking into her eyes as if offering her something.

But did she dare take it?

Chapter Nine

Erin heard the sound of a vehicle and despite knowing it was Saturday and that Dean wasn't coming to work today, either, she hurried to the window to see who it might be. But it was only a truck driving by on the road.

She wondered if she had chased him away the day they went riding. He had tried to be kind and she had overreacted.

Jan had phoned on Wednesday, full of apologies to tell her the windows had been delayed and could they come Monday instead. So Dean hadn't come by, either. Thursday he'd told her he was stopping by to pick up some tools and she had taken extra care with her clothes, putting on one of the new outfits. But then Lauren had called to ask if she could come to town for lunch with her and Jodie. So she'd met her sisters in town, but by the time she'd returned she realized Dean had come and gone while she was away.

He'd also told her he would help her measure the house for new flooring, but either he'd forgotten or was avoiding her. So to keep busy she had measured up the rooms herself and driven into town to order the flooring. She'd told herself repeatedly the past few days that she had done the right thing when they went riding. That her feelings for Dean were changing and she didn't want to encourage something that couldn't happen.

The sound of Caitlin fussing snapped Erin from her thoughts. She walked back to her bedroom. Her little girl had been out of sorts all morning, which was unusual for her. Caitlin lay crying in the crib, her arms waving, her tiny fingers curled into miniature fists, her legs kicking with little jerks.

"Oh, honey," Erin cooed, picking her up and holding her close. Caitlin immediately grew quiet, snuffling against Erin's neck, her tiny hands tangling in her mother's hair.

Erin frowned as she cuddled her. Her baby felt warmer than usual. Erin touched her head. Definitely warmer. The thermometer she had wasn't working properly so she had no way of checking if she was running a fever or not.

Should she take her to the doctor? Would it seem pointless? She wished she knew what to do. Jodie was in Great Falls today, and there was no answer when she called Lauren. She tried her aunt Laura's phone, but there was no response there, either.

Caitlin arched her back, growing more distressed, and Erin's concern grew. She pulled her phone out and did a quick search of fevers in babies, hoping to find something. Everything she read recommended medication and tepid baths.

Caitlin's cries became more frantic.

Should she bring her to the hospital? What if it was nothing?

Erin closed the browser on her phone and went to her contacts. Maybe Vic would know how to get a hold of Lauren. She dialed the number, holding Caitlin close, walking back and forth and growing more anxious with each step.

"Hello, this is Vic's phone, but it's Dean talking."

Erin's heart jumped into her throat. "Um…this is Erin…" She was disappointed how the simple sound of his voice could send her into a tailspin. "I need to talk to Lauren."

"She's not here. She and Vic went out and Vic left his phone behind."

"She's not answering her phone," Erin said, unable to keep the fear out of her voice.

"Are you okay? You sound worried."

"I'm fine. It…it's Caitlin."

"What about her? Is she okay?"

"I don't know. She's running a fever and I don't know how bad it is because the thermometer I bought doesn't register." She sucked in a quick breath realizing how panicky she sounded. "What kind of mother has a malfunctioning thermometer?"

"A mother who just moved and is probably still unpacking," Dean said.

His words made her feel better about herself. Just a little. "But still—"

"Are you at home? Do you want me to bring you to the doctor?"

"I don't know what to do." And for the first time since she had moved into this house located on an isolated corner of the ranch she understood her sisters' concern about her moving here. She should have found a place in town. Closer to the hospital. She was a terrible, selfish mother.

"I could drive myself."

"I'm sure you can, but if I drive you in you won't be distracted. Why don't I come anyway and bring you to the hospital. What do you think of that?"

Erin hesitated. It was a battle between a fear of and a deep yearning for seeing him again.

"I promise I won't try to kiss you," he added.

He sounded like he was teasing her, but his voice held a faint edge and she knew it was a response to her reaction to his kiss.

"I can drive myself," she repeated. But even as she bravely spoke the words she heard the faint tremble in her voice.

And Dean must have heard it, too.

"I'll be right there," he said, then ended the call.

Erin held Caitlin close, a mixture of emotions tumbling through her as she set her own phone down.

Dean was coming, after all.

She wanted to see him.

But at the same time, she didn't.

It's all for your daughter, she admonished herself.

And somehow that made her feel a bit better.

The smell of the hospital brought back too many bad memories for Dean.

He fidgeted in the hard leather chair just outside of Emergency, remembering too well the agonizing pain that had ripped through him the last time he was here.

He had been stabilized and from here it had been a speedy ambulance ride to Bozeman where he spent a month, then back here for the long haul of therapy and the slow recovery he had neglected.

Just as he formulated that thought, Mike Sawchuk, the very physiotherapist he'd been avoiding, strode down the hallway, his rubber shoes squeaking on the shining floor.

"Hey, Dean, what brings you here?" Mike stopped by Dean's chair, his hands shoved in the pockets of his track pants, the overhead lights gleaming off his shaved head. "Do I dare to hope you're here to make an appointment with me?"

Dean shifted uncomfortably under Mike's slightly mocking look. "I know I haven't followed up—"

"For the past couple months," Mike interrupted. He was grinning, but Dean heard the reprimand in his voice. "You know that you need to keep this up. You're going to lose mobility if you don't."

A myriad of excuses jumped forward, but Dean knew Mike would accept none of them.

"How has the leg been?" Mike asked, dropping into a chair across from him as if he had all the time in the world.

"Actually a bit better. I even went riding the other day."

"Really? That's progress."

While Mike would know about the pain riding caused, he had no idea of the fear. No one did.

Except Erin.

But he had gotten through that, as well.

On a plug horse Erin's baby could ride.

He dismissed the critical thought. It was still riding. A small step to be sure, but a step.

"But you still have to be careful to make sure you

don't have the wrong muscles overcompensating and causing problems down the road," Mike said. "I know you can feel like you're having some success now, but you need a comprehensive program to work all your muscle groups properly."

"I guess" was all Dean could muster. "I didn't feel like I was getting anywhere. It seemed pointless."

"Baby steps, if you'll pardon the expression." A hint of frustration entered Mike's voice. "Building a strong foundation to work off of. I'd like to see you come more often. Give me a chance to show you what can happen. Even though you rode that horse I'm sure it hurt and I'm sure you're feeling it yet."

Dean shifted awkwardly in his chair, as if in memory of the pain which kept him from working for a couple of days. He had felt pretty good after riding, but the next day he'd been hurting just as Mike had correctly assumed. He hadn't called Erin to tell her why he wasn't coming. He didn't want to recognize that part of it was the discomfort he felt, but a larger part was her reaction to his kiss.

"So, what do you say? Give me a decent chance to help you get more mobile?"

For some reason the sympathetic looks Erin had given him when he'd tried to get on the horse, when he'd had almost fallen in her living room, dropped into his brain. It still stung and he didn't want to see that again.

"Let me check my schedule" was all he was giving Mike for now.

"Taking physical therapy doesn't mean you're weak," Mike said, sounding even firmer than he had before. "It means you're smart."

Dean nodded at that, thinking of how happy Vic would be if he started therapy again. His brother had been nagging him for months to go back. To get riding again.

And if it made a difference?

Again his thoughts drifted to Erin.

"I'll call you next week," he said. "After I talk to my boss."

"Sounds good." Mike slapped his knees and then stood. "I can't fix everything, but I know we can get you walking better than you are now." Mike patted him on the shoulder, then walked away, whistling. Dean sighed as he watched him leave knowing he was in for a lot of work.

But if it helped?

He saw Mike slow down just as he saw Erin coming out of Emergency, holding Caitlin, wrapped in a light blanket, close to her chest. Mike stopped and seemed to be asking her something. Dean couldn't hear what they were saying, but it wasn't hard to miss the appreciative look on Mike's face. The physiotherapist lifted the blanket and smiled down at Caitlin, which bugged him more than he wanted to admit.

Then Erin laughed, which annoyed him further.

Dean slowly got to his feet, the ache in his muscles a reminder of what Mike had been saying and of his own limitations. He watched Mike saunter off, showcasing the obvious the difference between Dean and a healthier man.

The smile on Erin's face when she turned and saw Dean made him feel marginally better. She walked toward him, shifting her purse on her arm.

"What did the doctor say?" he asked, trying not to wince as he straightened out his leg.

"She's not running high fever. The doc figured it was just a cold, from a virus." She looked relieved. "But I should stop at the drugstore and pick up some medication and a new thermometer for her. If that's okay."

He nodded at her but couldn't get the sight of her and Mike out of his brain.

"So how do you know Sawchuk?"

"Michael?" Her soft smile didn't bode well for his own presence of mind. "I remember him from church. He led a Bible study I went to the summers I was here."

Of course he did, Dean thought, stifling a flash of annoyance.

Seriously, how could he be irritated with a guy who led Bible study? How petty was he?

When it came to Erin, he realized he didn't like comparing himself to Mike and being found wanting in so many ways.

"He's a physical therapist in the hospital here," Dean added, trying to be generous.

"I remember him talking about that," Erin said. Caitlin was crying again and Erin shot her daughter a look of concern.

"We should probably get that medicine for her," Dean offered.

"Yeah. I think so." As they walked toward the entrance, Erin slowed her steps to match Dean's—adding another layer to his insecurity—and put her hand on his arm. "Thanks so much for bringing me. I feel a bit foolish, seeing as how it was really nothing important, but I'm much more at ease now that she's seen the doctor."

"Then I'm glad I could help," he said, trying not to read more into her gentle touch than simple gratitude.

But as they walked together back to his truck he knew his feelings for Erin were becoming more difficult to sort out the more time he spent with her.

Chapter Ten

The gathering dusk closing in created a tiny cocoon in the cab of Dean's truck.

The radio played country music, a quiet counterpoint to the hum of the tires on the pavement and the faint snuffling coming from Caitlin tucked in her seat in the back. Dean had kindly waited while Erin opened the baby medicine they had just bought and gave some to Caitlin right away. It seemed to be working because she had stopped fussing about ten minutes ago.

"I think she's settling," Dean was saying, shooting a glance across the darkening cab.

The lights from the dashboard threw his features into interesting hollows and crags, highlighting how good-looking he really was.

Erin felt a curl of appreciation as he looked back to the road again. She had always thought he was attractive, but time had matured him and made him more handsome.

"Thanks again for driving me and for taking me to the pharmacy," she said, relieved now that they were on their way back home and she knew Caitlin was okay.

"I wasn't that busy anyhow. I was just glad I answered Vic's phone when I did."

"Me, too."

They rode in silence for a few more miles, Erin clutching her purse and the bag from the pharmacy, feeling suddenly tongue-tied and shy.

He'd had the ability to do this to her in the past, but now her reticence was because of her shifting emotions. Bringing her and Caitlin to the hospital meant more to her than she wanted to acknowledge. It was what a friend did and thinking of Dean as a friend was disconcerting.

Dean reached over and turned the music up and it filled the silence hanging between them for the rest of the way to her place.

When they got to the house he turned the truck off and got out. Erin managed to get Caitlin's car seat out of the clips that held it secure and then Dean was beside her.

"Let me take something," he said, indicating her purse and the bags she was trying to juggle. While they were at the pharmacy she'd bought some diapers and a few other baby supplies.

She wanted to protest that she could manage, but it was nice to have help so she handed Dean the bags and she took her purse and the car seat.

Erin couldn't help the twinge of embarrassment she felt when she turned on a light and looked over her house. Her computer sat on the coffee table with a few rough sketches torn out of her sketchpad beside it. A basket of laundry, waiting to be folded, was pushed up against the couch. Dishes sat piled up on the counter in the kitchen and her blender, still rimed with leftover smoothie, sat in the sink.

"Sorry about the mess," she murmured as she carried Caitlin into the living room.

"Looks cozy," Dean said following her, bags rustling as he laid them on the kitchen table. "Lived-in."

Erin set the car seat on the floor and her daughter immediately expressed her displeasure. She quickly undid the buckles, laying the back of her hand against Caitlin's forehead as she slowly settled. Still warm but not as bad as before.

She was about to take her out of the car seat when her cell phone rang.

She glanced at the screen, her heart skipping a beat when she saw the number. It was the client she had been wooing for the past half year. A small publishing company that had just started up and was looking for someone to do marketing materials for them.

Caitlin started complaining just as she connected to take the call.

She answered the phone, fumbling one-handed with the clasp on Caitlin's car seat. "Hello, Erin McCauley here," she said, hoping she didn't sound as breathless as she felt.

"So glad we could finally connect," an unfamiliar voice said on the other end, speaking so loudly Erin had to hold the phone away from her ear. "Do you have some time to talk?"

She didn't really, she thought as Caitlin began crying again, but she wasn't about to tell a prospective client that.

Then Dean was beside her, brushing her hands gently away, motioning for her to take the call somewhere else. Erin shook her head, but he pulled the car seat away, taking the decision out of her hands.

"I'll take care of her," he whispered.

Erin was about to protest, but he shooed her away. So she went into her bedroom to take the call.

Dean watched as Erin headed toward her bedroom, her phone clamped to her ear. Just before she closed the door behind her she glanced over at him. He gave her a thumbs-up and an encouraging smile.

"So, I guess it's just you and me for now," Dean said looking down at Caitlin, who was staring up at him as if wondering who her mother had left her with now.

She looked tiny in the car seat, held in by straps wider than her arms. Then she waved her hands, sticking out her feet, and her mouth curled up in protest. She whimpered and looked like she was about to cry. He guessed she wanted to come out of the car seat.

So he began the complicated task of figuring out how to unbuckle this little mite from the contraption. He fought with the straps, fighting down his frustration. He knew how to throw a double diamond hitch on a packhorse, rig up a running martingale, saddle up a rangy bronc in a metal bucking chute, but this set of straps and buckles confounded him.

"I don't suppose you can help me out," he muttered as Caitlin let out another squawk. He didn't want to interrupt Erin. She had looked so excited when the call had come through and he guessed it had something to do with the work she did from her home.

He looked at the harness from a few angles, trying not to feel pressured by baby's screwed-up face and flailing arms. He pushed on a button and, yahtzee, there it was. One of the straps came unclipped. Moving quickly now he pulled the other one free and then, finally, lifted a squirming and somewhat upset little girl out of the seat.

She felt so tiny, like she was just a bundle of bones and skin. Other than a puppy, he had never held anything this small.

Not sure what to do, he rocked her slowly, walking over to the couch.

He sat down, swung his legs up and lay back easing out a sigh of relief. He adjusted Caitlin, hoping he didn't hurt her as he shifted her arms and legs. She laid her head in the crook of his neck, her snuffling cries quieting.

"I got the touch," he murmured as he felt her melt against him.

She still felt overly warm, but she didn't appear to be distressed. He wondered if she needed a diaper change but figured mastering the car seat was enough for now.

Caitlin lifted her head and it wobbled as she looked at him, her lips pursed in a perfect cupid's bow. Her eyes crossed and then her head dropped again, her one hand inching upward. Her minuscule fingers latched onto his shirt and as he snuggled her close he felt a melting in his heart.

How could such a tiny person tug so easily on his soul? And so quickly?

He brushed his cheek over the downy fluff that was her hair, surprised at how sweet she smelled.

He'd never held a baby before, but somehow he felt comfortable with her. Maybe he was better at this than he thought.

She moved a bit, then her breathing became more even and in minutes she was asleep.

Her warmth, the amazing feeling of her in his arms created an unforeseen softness in his heart.

I could get used to this.

But no sooner did that thought slip into his mind than his musings shifted to Erin. She hadn't exactly encouraged his kiss, but, as he mulled it over for about the hundredth time since it happened, she hadn't exactly discouraged it, either. And behind that belief crept the vague hope that things were changing between them.

Did he dare allow that?

He looked down at Caitlin now sleeping on his chest, one tiny hand curled up beside her face, her lashes a faint shadow against her round cheek. This little munchkin came with Erin. She was part of the package and an extra responsibility he couldn't treat lightly.

Could he do this? Could he take this on?

Then she sighed lightly, her fingers twitching, and again a surprising wave of affection came over him. And with that, he had another reason to try to get his mobility back.

Chapter Eleven

The client, Gretchen Shorey, was effusive about the samples Erin had sent, and complimented her on her versatility. Erin had sent a couple of mock-ups of some book covers. One was for a nonfiction self-help book, the other a dystopian novel for young adults. Plus some basic ad concepts for marketing connected to the books.

"I'm so glad you like them," Erin said, feeling a rush of pleasure at the praise. She hadn't done much work the past half year and was afraid she had lost her edge and connections.

She'd gotten this opportunity from a fellow graphic artist she was friends with on Facebook, who had turned down a chance to work for them. Her friend had encouraged Erin to send some samples and cold-call, and here she was.

"Love them. Fantastic work. So, what we're look-ing at is print as well as ebook. Got to cover all the angles these days," Gretchen said with a quick laugh. "We're just starting out and don't have a huge lineup. I can't promise you all the covers but I do have some connections to a tech company which might be looking for ad work as well."

At her words Erin felt a surge of hope for future work. She didn't want to tell her sisters that she had been a bit concerned. It would make her look irresponsible but this affirmation made her relax her unease.

They talked details and compensation and Erin grew even more positive. When she finally ended the call she held onto the phone a moment as if to cement what had just happened.

Thank you, Lord, were the first words that slipped into her mind as she released a long, slow breath, looking around the room. Her eyes fell on the clock first then Caitlin's crib. She realized with a start that in the excitement and the pleasure of talking shop for the past twenty minutes, she had forgotten about her daughter.

She shoved her phone into the back pocket of her blue jeans and yanked open the door of her bedroom.

But she couldn't see either Dean or Caitlin. Heart pounding now she rushed to the front door, passing the couch on her way.

What she saw there made her come to a halt.

Dean lay on the couch, his head on the armrest, his legs stretched out along the length of the couch. Caitlin lay curled like a ball on his chest, his arms curved around her.

Both were asleep.

Erin stood over them, her breath quickening at the picture of her daughter in Dean's arms. The planes of his face had softened, his mouth was relaxed, his head angled toward Caitlin's. He looked like he was protecting her and the sight made Erin's heart hitch.

Dean, a man she had never thought of as fatherly,

looked so comfortable and at ease. As if he had done this many times before.

She thought back to Sam, Caitlin's real father, and how faithless he had been to his own child. The child in his wife's arms when she'd come to see Erin.

Don't think about that. You didn't know.

But here was Dean, holding her daughter while he slept.

A quick glance at her watch showed her that it was getting on to 5:00. Supper time. She had pulled out a casserole Lauren had delivered yesterday and had figured on heating it up.

Should she ask Dean to stay?

She shrugged off the question, trying not to let herself read too much into the situation. He had brought her to town—the least she could do was feed him.

As the casserole warmed up in the oven she set the table for two, feeling a hint of intimacy as she laid the plates out across from each other. Was she presuming too much? Would he want to stay? It wasn't like she'd been the most cordial to him.

She pushed the thoughts aside and grabbed cutlery. Just a simple dinner with old friends. Yet even as she told herself that, another part of her mocked that idea. Dean had never been a "friend."

She busied herself in the kitchen, feeling rather domestic. A man holding her sleeping baby on the couch while she made supper. Like a little family.

The thought snuck up on her as she cut up vegetables for the salad and try as she might, she couldn't dislodge it. Because with that thought came the memory of Dean's kiss—something else she hadn't been able to dismiss.

She heard a groan, then a heavy sigh and she guessed Dean was waking up.

"Hey, little girl," she heard him mutter. "Is your mommy still yapping on the phone?"

She smiled at that, unable to take offense at his comment because she could hear the underlying humor in his tone.

Then she heard another groan and wondered if his leg bothered him. She hurried over to the couch just as he sat up, still holding Caitlin. He grimaced as he did so and her suspicions were confirmed.

"Here, let me help you," she said, reaching out to take Caitlin from him.

She was surprised when he didn't protest. But before he handed over her daughter, he brushed his cheek over her head. It was such a small thing and if she hadn't been watching she would have missed it.

But it landed in her heart and stuck there.

She eased Caitlin out of his arms, and holding her close, brought her to her bedroom, gently laying her down in the crib.

As she looked down she felt a pang of vulnerability blended with a fierce protectiveness. Caitlin had only Erin to take care of her. She depended on her fully.

While her feelings for Dean were changing she knew she had to be careful.

Yet, in spite of her self-talk, as she closed the door behind her and saw Dean standing in her living room she felt an eager anticipation.

"That was delicious," Dean said, wiping his mouth with a napkin. He folded it up and set it on his plate, shooting a cautious smile over at Erin. "Thanks for having me."

When she'd invited him to stay for supper his first reaction was to say no. But the welcoming smile on her face made him change his mind. That and the fact that she said she'd wanted to pay him back for helping her out.

Balancing the scales he understood.

"You're welcome." She fiddled with her knife, moving it to one side of her plate then another. Then she glanced over at him again. "It was nice to have company for dinner, though I can't claim any credit. Lauren made the casserole."

"She's a good sister."

"She and Jodie both are, in their own ways, though they do like to boss me around." Erin fiddled a bit more with her knife.

"She has that ability," Dean said with a grin. "But in the end it worked out good." Then he caught himself, realizing how that sounded. "I mean, for me. For riding," he amended quickly. "I hadn't been on a horse since and I was scared and—"

Erin reached over and put her hand on his arm. "I know what you were saying." But she kept her hand there. "And I appreciate what you told me. About being afraid. That can't have been easy to admit."

"Always been told to cowboy up," he said with a short laugh.

"I never did understand what that meant or where it came from. I mean, why up? Why not down?"

Dean laughed. "Not sure myself. It gets tossed around at rodeos so much no one every really stops to think about it. Anyhow, it took a depressing amount of cowboy upping to get on that old nag Jodie picked out for me."

"I think you showed more courage getting on that old nag, who just so happened to be a horse I used to ride, than getting on any saddle bronc you've ever ridden."

"I don't know about that," he said, standing to clear the table. "But I'll just say thanks."

She smiled and got up, as well.

He brought his plate to the counter and then returned for the rest.

"You don't have to stay to help with the dishes. I'm sure you've got things you need to do," she said, setting the half-full casserole dish on the counter.

He did have to get back to the ranch to help Vic with the tractor that had broken down yesterday when they were loading up bales for Monty Bannister. And his mom wanted him to help her clear out her greenhouse.

But he wanted to prolong this time with Erin. Vic could clean up the clogged fuel line on his own. And the greenhouse could wait.

"Not really. I don't mind to help."

"I don't have a dishwasher," she warned him.

All the better.

"Just another chance for me to cowboy up," he joked.

She chuckled, which made him feel better than it should.

"So did you make up your mind about your flooring?" he said as he scraped the dishes while she took care of the leftovers. "I said I was coming to help you measure…" He let the sentence trail off. He felt bad, but after Tuesday he needed to retreat and lick his wounds.

"That's okay. I figured it out myself. And I got it ordered already."

"Wow, you're efficient."

"I've learned to do things for myself."

Her comment raised another blitz of questions and curiosity about her life before she came back to Saddlebank. "You said that you rehabbed a house?" he asked as he set the plates aside.

"With my roommates, yes. And Sam."

"Is that what he did for a living?" He knew he was pushing his luck, but he felt a need to know more about this shadowy figure who was, hopefully, part of Erin's past.

"No. Nothing like that. He's a doctor. Surgeon in fact."

Dean shoved the stopper in the sink, nodding. Surgeon. Rich, probably.

"And if you're wondering why I left him, well, I got pregnant and he didn't want Caitlin and…there were other reasons."

He turned to her, hearing the understated pain in her voice. And though he wondered what those "other reasons" were, it didn't matter. She sounded sad.

"That must have been hard," he said, turning on the taps to fill the sink.

"I was the one who ended the relationship." Erin set the casserole in the fridge, then closed the door, her back to him. "Things hadn't been great before… before I got pregnant. But…" Her voice broke and she lowered her head. Dean, unsure of what to do, took a chance and walked over to her. He put his hand on her shoulder to comfort her.

She straightened as if gathering strength from a place he supposed she had drawn from before.

"Sorry," she said, her voice matter-of-fact.

"You don't have to apologize," he said, keeping his voice quiet as if to encourage her to entrust him with what she held back.

She turned to him then, a wry smile on her face. "I have got to stop making a habit of getting all sappy in front of you. I guess it's just with Caitlin and all…"

Her voice trailed away as she looked up at him, her soft blue eyes locked on his. They stood close enough that he could smell the scent of her shampoo, catch the faint smudge of mascara under her lower lashes.

"You're feeling vulnerable," he finished for her.

"That and…other things."

It was the breathy way she spoke those words, the way she kept her eyes on his that raised his hopes and ignited old dreams.

In spite of his promise not to kiss her again, he lowered his head, pausing within inches of her lips as if to give her the opportunity to pull away. Instead, she closed the distance between them.

Their lips met, warm and soft, a connection that shook him to his core. He held her mouth against his for a few more seconds and then she gently drew back.

He rested his forehead against her, her face a delightful blur.

"So, this changes things," he said, his voice quiet as if he didn't want to disturb the moment.

"Yes. It does," she returned. He heard her swallow and then, regretfully, she lowered her hand and drew back, resting against the door of the refrigerator, her hands now at her sides.

He pulled back as well, trying to get a read from her expression. Her lips held a smile and though she looked down he caught a sparkle in her eyes, a crinkle at the corners.

"I know this is a complication for you," he said, preferring to voice her potential objections.

"I do have Caitlin to think of," she said, acknowledging where he was going.

"And her father?" he prompted, needing to get that much out of the way before they moved in the direction he thought they might be headed.

"Like I told you, not in the picture."

"I'm glad to hear that," he said. "I'm not so sure I want to share."

She sucked in a quick breath, her eyes shooting to his.

"Really?"

"Yeah, really."

"Well, it was a bad relationship that was a mistake. The only good thing that came of that mess was Caitlin." Her quiet vehemence made him wonder if there was more to the situation. Right now, however, he didn't want to know. Because talking about Caitlin's father brought him into the present and Dean wanted him planted firmly in Erin's past.

But he did want to fix the regret and bitterness in her voice.

"I know how easy it is to make mistakes," he said. "I've learned a lot about God's grace and how He helps us work through those missteps in life."

She looked up at him, frowning, and he wondered if she was going to, once again, push any talk of God aside.

"You sound so wise."

"You sound so surprised."

Her laughter made him feel good.

"Anything I know now was hard-won," he said, fingering a strand of hair back from her face, tucking it behind her ear. "I learned how valuable life is and not to mess around with it. That and to let go of my pride."

He thought of his chat with Mike and how long it had taken him to admit he needed the man's help. But as he looked down at Erin he knew he had another reason to improve his life.

"We have that in common, then," she said, touching his hand with hers.

"How so?"

She twined her fingers through his in a gesture that spoke of a comfortable familiarity. "I struggled with pride, too. I was ashamed to come back here, a single mother. My sisters and I have always had our roles. Jodie was always the rebel. Lauren was always the responsible one. But me, I was always the good girl. The one that reminded them to go to church, to read their Bible. To stay close to God." She released a short laugh. "So you need to understand how hard it was to come back to them not only a single mother but someone who had strayed from the faith she had encouraged them to follow."

"But you know you can always go back," he said. "And if God accepts a selfish and cocky cowboy like me I know He will take back someone like you. Someone who is so—"

She put her fingers on his lips as if to forestall anything else he might say. "Please, don't say it again."

He didn't, knowing that it would make her upset.

"Come to church" was all he said instead.

"I'll think about it."

He wanted to say more but he gave in to an impulse and kissed her again, cupping her face in his hands.

And when he looked into her eyes he caught a shadow of pain that made him wonder yet again what she wasn't telling him.

Though he wanted to know now he also knew she had to learn to trust him.

He just hoped that what she was holding back wasn't something that could break the tender relationship growing between them.

Chapter Twelve

Erin stood with Caitlin in her arms in the back of the church, firmly in the grip of second thoughts, as she looked over the scattered congregation.

Her sisters weren't here yet. They had promised they would meet her and sit with her, but she didn't see them.

She regretted the impulse she had given in to this morning. It was because of Dean she was here. His gently spoken invitation to come to church was a surprise, but it was also encouraging.

Her aunt Laura was playing the piano, the sounds of the familiar hymn making Erin smile.

She looked down at Caitlin, wondering again if she should have brought her to church. According to the digital thermometer Dean had insisted on buying for her, her fever was down. He had checked her a number of times, apparently fascinated with how the thermometer worked. Erin had, however, drawn the line on Dean pasting a bug-shaped fever patch he had purchased on Caitlin's forehead that would give a readout of her temperature. He'd tossed those in the shopping cart, as well.

She stroked Caitlin's soft cheek, smiling at the memory of her little shopping trip with Dean yesterday. He'd acted like a fussy old grandma as he read every label of every product making sure she bought exactly the right kind.

"Erin. Welcome to the services."

She looked up as Brooke Dillon came up beside her, laying her hand on Erin's shoulder. Behind her slouched George Bamford, the owner of the Grill and Chill. He gave Erin a quick uptick of his chin, which, she guessed, was his version of hello. "Nice hair," Brooke said with a grin.

"Thanks again. I really like it."

Brooke fluffed Erin's hair, then fluttered her hands in an apologetic gesture. "Sorry. Habit. Is Lauren or Jodie here?"

"Not yet, but I'm early."

"You can come and sit with us, if you want."

The offer eased away her misgivings about coming to church today. "Thanks so much, but I think I'll wait."

"And here's your enchanting little girl." Brooke fingered the blanket away from Caitlin's face, smiling that tender smile women reserved for little babies. "We do have a nursery downstairs."

"I know, but I felt too nervous bringing her there. Besides, she hasn't been feeling well so I want to keep her close."

"And she's such a good baby. If she can sleep through all the noise in the beauty shop, I'm sure she'll sleep just fine with your aunt Laura playing." Brooke's mouth fell open, her eyes wide with alarm. "I mean, she'll sleep well. Not that your aunt is a boring player or anything. Just quieter than the group we usually have. They're pretty loud in comparison, that's all I was trying—"

"She gets it," George interrupted, putting his hand on Brooke's shoulder. He angled Erin a questioning look. "Right?"

"I knew what you meant," she assured Brooke with a smile.

"Let's sit down," George added.

But before he left he paused to look down at Caitlin, who still slept. "Cute kid," he said tersely.

Then he took Brooke's arm and together they walked down the aisle to an empty seat.

Erin grinned as she watched George step aside to let Brooke sit down. As soon as he was settled he draped his arm over Brooke's shoulder. *Guess it's official*, she thought. Sitting in church together showed as much of a commitment as an engagement ring.

When her phone buzzed, Erin jumped, feeling guilty for not turning it off. She finagled it one-handed out of her purse and thumbed the screen to life, frowning as she saw Lauren's name. "Hello," she said walking toward the door, speaking quietly as she sat down on an empty chair just near the door.

"It's Lauren," Erin heard her sister say in a tone of disgust. "And big surprise, we'll be late. Finn's working so we took Jodie's car and it broke down, another big surprise." She heard a laughing comment in the background. Jodie probably. Then Lauren was talking, her own voice muffled. "I don't care. I told you we should have let Vic pick us up."

Erin heard a sassy rejoinder and smiled as her sisters lobbed snide comments back and forth.

"So you're saying I should just go in by myself?" she asked, hoping to catch Lauren's attention.

"I know you wanted us there for you and I'm sorry that we can't be." She sounded so contrite, but edged with that was frustration with their flighty younger sister.

"I'm a big girl."

"I know you are," Lauren said, "But I also know you were hoping we could be there to support you."

"I'll be fine."

They made plans for after church. They were going to have lunch and then work on decorations for Jodie and Finn's wedding, which was coming up in a couple of months. Erin said goodbye, then turned her phone off and dropped it in her oversize purse-slash-diaper bag. She shrugged her purse over her shoulder, adjusting the blanket around her baby.

People walked past her, smiling in greeting. She didn't recognize any of them and she wondered if she should go in.

But it would look silly if she left now.

She smoothed one hand over her skirt, checking it again. She hadn't worn it since she got pregnant. In fact, she was pleased it still fit. The skirt had been an impulse buy when Sam had canceled one of their dates. Again.

Erin looked down at her daughter, feeling a twinge of sorrow at the life she was giving her. Erin had always hoped to have a husband who loved her and respected her. A man she would be faithful to, unlike her own mother. They were going to have three, maybe four kids. Live in a house out in the country so she could have the chickens she always wanted. The outdoor clothesline. Maybe a horse or two for her children.

She pushed down the thoughts, relegating them to the same place she had put other dreams that had died. Her mom and dad back together again and all of them on the ranch that she loved so much.

Caitlin yawned, her tiny mouth opening so wide Erin thought it had to hurt. Then she shifted around and opened her eyes zeroing in on Erin.

I'll take care of you, little bug, she thought, smiling down at her precious daughter. *I promise*.

She was about to walk back to the entrance to the sanctuary when the door behind her opened, bringing with it the cooling air of the approaching fall.

She turned and there was Dean.

He wore a plain white shirt and dark jeans that rode low on his hips, cinched with a leather belt holding a simple buckle. His hair was still damp and his cheeks shone from being freshly shaved. And when he saw her his smile lit up his face.

"Hey, there, you came." He walked over to her in his now-familiar hitching step. He stopped beside her, towering over her, smiling down. "And how's the babe?" Without waiting to hear an update he laid the back of his hand on Caitlin's tiny forehead, dwarfing it. "She feels good, though it's hard to say without a fever bug on her forehead."

He sounded so serious, but when Erin met his gaze she caught a twitch of his lips and a wrinkling at the corner of his eyes.

"That fancy thermometer you bought works great." she retorted. "I don't need to slap sticky bugs on her head."

"I think a little frog would go perfectly with that blanket," he said, curling it around Caitlin's arm.

His gentle touches, light adjustments of Caitlin's blanket and the way he looked down at her dove almost as deeply into her soul as his kisses had.

Her cheeks warmed at the memory of that gently smiling mouth on hers. She knew she was falling for him. That he was becoming more and more important every day.

She just wished she knew how to proceed.

"By the way, Vic called," Dean continued, looking back at her. "He's on his way to rescue your sisters. So if you want to wait for them we can."

Erin knew the service would start in less than five minutes. She didn't want to disrupt it by coming in late.

"No. Let's go in."

As soon as she spoke the words she felt silly. As if she assumed that Dean would be with her.

But he just nodded and together they found a seat close to the back.

And as they did, Erin felt a surprising peace.

That peace had nothing to do with sitting beside Dean, she tried to tell herself. Or his arm brushing hers. Or that she felt, for the first time in over a year, that her life was falling into a good place.

The words of the songs Aunt Laura was playing were projected on the large screen at the front of the church and a sense of homecoming washed over her.

The song was an old favorite of hers and she wondered if Aunt Laura had chosen it or if it was simply a coincidence.

"My comfort is in You, Lord. As long as life goes

on, in life and death, with every breath, I call You the risen Son."

She felt a prickling in her throat as she sang the words in a church she had attended as a young girl and then as a teenager. And now she was here, many years later, holding her child in her arms. The prodigal daughter.

Her voice broke on the second verse that spoke of God's yearning faithfulness and how He calls and waits to *"...wipe away tears and calm deepest fears and erase our every stain."* She thought of how far she had strayed, of promises she had broken and caused to be broken. The stains on her own life.

But this old song with its promises of a faithful, loving God whom she had known in a different time of her life and who, she knew deep in her soul, still loved her as she was at this moment, permeated her lonely, parched soul.

Dean knew he was supposed to keep his attention on the pastor, but it was difficult with Erin sitting right beside him. He knew he took a chance asking her to come sit with him especially with her holding her baby. He knew people would wonder and talk just as they had when he first started attending church. Not just about Erin coming back to Saddlebank as a single mother, but about Erin and Dean sitting together in church.

That was usually reserved for the postengagement part of any relationship. Like Brooke and George.

Always was a rebel, he thought, adjusting his hips to compensate for a growing cramp in his leg.

Tomorrow he was calling Mike to set up a schedule of appointments. He had hesitated, balking at the time it would take him away from work, but he also felt a renewed sense of purpose. And it was all thanks to the beautiful woman sitting beside him.

He glanced over at Erin, who was looking down at Caitlin. Her features possessed a serenity that tugged at his heart. She reminded him of his own mother who was so caring, so loving. Who, he knew, had prayed daily that he would come back to faith.

He smiled just as Erin looked up at him, their eyes holding again. Then she looked away to the pastor.

"Grace is a word that, unlike many other church words like charity or love or faithfulness, has stood the test of time," Pastor Dykstra was saying. "Grace still lingers in our vocabulary as a touchstone for the undeserved. For something received, given freely. The only catch is we have to reach out and take it." Pastor Dykstra paused there as if to give his congregation time to ponder this thought.

Dean knew this as well, but hearing the pastor speak of grace while sitting beside the girl who was, at one time, someone so unreachable made the notion of that same grace all the more real and true.

He didn't deserve Erin. But somehow, in some weird and strange way, they had found each other at this point in their lives.

He knew he didn't deserve her any more than he deserved God's grace. Both were a gift and he knew he was foolish not to take it.

Chapter Thirteen

"She's so adorable. Look at her tiny hands." Ellen Bannister let Caitlin's finger curl around hers as she smiled down at the baby, the light reflecting off her glasses as she sat down beside Erin in the pew.

The service was over and Ellen, who had been sitting across the aisle from her and Dean, had come over as soon as the last song was done, shooing Dean away so she could sit beside Erin.

The wrinkles near her friendly eyes deepened as Ellen smiled at Caitlin. From her memories of the older woman, Erin knew the lines around her mouth came from laughter. "She is such a gift, you know." Erin heard the sincerity in her voice and, slowly, as other women came to them, she felt as if she was cocooned in caring and acceptance and, for lack of a better word, grace.

The minister's words settled in her soul as she looked around the gathered women, all of various ages. All smiling at her. All accepting her.

Why had she been so hesitant to come?

Then she felt a hug from behind and a hand on her

shoulder and she turned to see her sisters standing there.

"Sorry we were late. We sat farther back," Jodie said, bending over Erin to look at her niece. "Hey, baby girl, were you good for your mommy?"

"Thank goodness Vic was able to pick us up or we'd never have gotten here," Lauren complained.

"We could have hitchhiked," Jodie murmured, unperturbed by Lauren's annoyance.

"Right. On a Sunday. Like we'd get picked up."

Erin had to smile at her sisters' exchange, remembering other times when their bickering would be irritating. Now it was familiar. It was home.

"Loved your playing this morning," one of the ladies gathered around was saying as Aunt Laura came to join them. Laura just smiled, her attention focused on Caitlin as she sat down on the other side of her niece and gave her a quick hug.

"So good to see you here," she said, her hands lingering on Erin's face as she held her gaze.

"I loved the one song you played."

Aunt Laura just smiled and gave her another hug. "I know you liked it."

So she had chosen it for her.

"And I'm looking forward to you girls joining me for lunch," she said, looking at Jodie and Lauren, as well. "And your young men."

"Finn is working," Jodie said with an exaggerated pout.

"Well, how about Vic and his younger brother, Dean?" She looked back at Erin with a conspiratorial smile and Erin knew that Aunt Laura had seen her sitting with Dean.

"Great idea," Jodie said. "I mean, he's going to practically be family once Lauren and Vic get married."

"Hardly," Lauren put in, still sounding confused. "He's going to be my brother-in-law."

"And you're our sister," Jodie said in a tone that seemed to say that was the end of that.

Half an hour later, the five of them were sitting around a large wooden table tucked in one corner of Aunt Laura's apartment above the flower shop.

"It's just soup and buns," she said with an apologetic tone as she set a large, dented pot on the table.

"Smells good for just soup and buns," Vic said, giving her a charming smile.

Was Aunt Laura simpering? Erin had to chuckle. Not that she blamed her. With his dark slashing brows, deep brown eyes and strong jaw, Vic was one appealing man.

Though Erin found her gaze drifting more to Dean than his brother. She was pleased he had accepted her aunt's invitation to join them for lunch. But while it meant she could spend more time with him, she felt bad for him because it also meant that time was spent under the watchful eyes of her sisters and aunt.

"Did Caitlin settle down okay?" her aunt asked as Jodie set a plate of buns on the table, then sat down to join them.

"She did. And how could she not in such a pretty room." Erin was touched that her aunt had a room set up for her baby. A crib complete with a mobile and a pink bedding set took up one corner and a change table was pushed along a wall. Both were a soft ivory and looked brand-new. One wall was papered in a green-

and-white striped paper and pink-and-green balls of tissue hung from the ceiling in one corner of the room.

It gave her a peculiar feeling. The same feeling she'd experienced at church this morning and in Brooke's hair salon. She'd thought she would have to come back to Saddlebank humiliated and ashamed, but it seemed that the people of the town were far more welcoming than she had given them credit for.

Aunt Laura just smiled and shrugged off the compliment, then she looked around the table. "This is so lovely," she said, a hitch in her voice. "I surely didn't think that all my girls would come back home. And settle down here."

This engendered more smiles and a gentle murmuring of assent. Then just before Aunt Laura bowed her head to pray, Erin shot a quick glance across the table at Dean. She was disconcerted to see him looking intently at her.

Just as he had in church.

She couldn't look away, nor did she want to. Feelings uncertain and new arced between them and with that came a sense of anticipation. Of waiting.

And more than ever Erin looked forward to tomorrow when Dean would be helping her in the house. And there wouldn't be anyone else around.

"I'm so glad we took out that carpet on Tuesday," Erin said as she handed Dean another board. "I still can't believe how much gunk there was underneath it."

"You'll be happy once this is done, I'm sure," Dean replied, slowly getting to his feet.

Jan had shown up on Monday with his crew and by the end of the day the new windows were in and the siding patched up. Erin felt as if she were closer to being ready for the winter that was slinking around the corner.

Tuesday they had ripped out the carpet and they started on the flooring on Wednesday. Today was Friday and they were still working on it. It could have been done quicker, but Dean had left every afternoon for physiotherapy.

She had to admit she'd been a touch flattered when Dean's therapist had flirted with her at the hospital.

But he wasn't her type.

She looked at the cowboy across the room, a man who at one time she hadn't considered her type, either. As he laid the last bit of carpet on the pile she saw a grimace creep across his face and guessed that between all the work and the extra physio he was hurting. But she knew Dean wouldn't appreciate it if she said anything.

Erin grabbed a broom and began sweeping up all the dirt that lay on the subfloor. "I'm so glad I never laid Caitlin down on the floor. Who knows what kind of germs and grossness she would have inhaled," she said.

"It's been here a few years," Dean said with a wry look as he stretched. He glanced around the house, his hand in the small of his back. "You put a few more pictures up since yesterday," he said.

She nodded, glancing over at some of the artwork she had done when she took her graphics art course in Nashville. "Just some stuff I've dragged around in my travels."

He walked over to a sketch, in which her father was kneeling down by a newborn calf, still holding the reins of his horse, who stood obediently and quietly behind him.

"That's a great picture," he said, his hands resting on his hips.

"One of the few tender moments I got to see in my dad," she said.

"Keith was a tough guy." Dean gave her a wry look. "I got to be on the receiving end of a few tongue lashings from him in my heyday. Every time he pulled me over I got the lecture."

"I can imagine."

"I'm sure he told you lots of stories about me."

She heard the faintly defensive tone in his voice and shook her head, slanting him a smile that she hoped showed him it didn't matter anymore. "Dad never said much about the people he dealt with. Though he was a demanding father, he was a principled man."

The closest he ever got to bringing anything home from work was to warn her to be careful who she went out with, glaring at her over his reading glasses, his bushy eyebrows bristling.

"It mustn't have been easy for you girls. Coming back here for a few months every summer and then going back to Knoxville." Dean took the dustpan from her, caught her by the hand and helped her to her feet. Except he didn't let go right away.

Erin looked down at their twined hands, smiling at the sight. It seemed so normal now. The past few days had been a slow movement together in the same direction. The delightful beginnings of a new relationship.

She considered his question as she tightened her grip on his hand. "My sisters didn't enjoy it that much, but I liked it. I missed the ranch when my mother left my father."

Dean was quiet a moment, then set the dustpan aside, catching her by the other hand. "So why did your mother leave?"

Erin hadn't been there that day when her father had ordered her mother and the girls off the ranch. But she'd heard about it from Jodie. Whispers under bedcovers in their grandmother's house in Knoxville. Quiet conversations away from their mother who grew more withdrawn every day.

"My parents didn't have a happy marriage. Aunt Laura told my sisters that Mom got pregnant with me and Lauren before they were married so Dad stepped up to his responsibilities. He cut short his dream of becoming a marine and became a deputy instead. I guess things just went downhill from there." Erin was disappointed at how her voice faltered, but she pushed on. "In the last years of their marriage Mom was cheating on him and when Dad found out, he told her to leave. Apparently there was even a time when Dad suspected Jodie wasn't his daughter."

"And you girls? Didn't he want you to stay with him?"

"I don't know. My mother never talked about it and she never sent us here. That happened after she died. Our grandmother thought Dad should take responsibility, and sent us here over the summer. I didn't mind as much as my sisters did. I enjoyed being on the ranch." She glanced over at the picture. "I loved going out with Dad to check the cows when they were calving. We'd ride all day, say practically nothing to each other, but it was a time of closeness that Lauren and Jodie never

had with him. But he was still a complicated man."
She thought of the letter he had written to her full of
apologies and regrets.

Dean tipped her chin up with his finger and as she
looked into his eyes she saw understanding, which
slowly warmed to something else entirely. When he
kissed her again, her hands clung to his, as if to an-
chor herself. Then he drew back and smiled. "I hope
I'm not a complicated man."

She heard the underlying tone in his voice. The unspoken question.

He wasn't complicated, but he did create a complication. Working a man into her life wasn't as easy as
it once was. She now had Caitlin to think of.

But behind that warning came the memory of Dean
holding her baby. How happy he was that Sam wasn't
involved in their lives.

This could work, she thought. This could happen.

And it was that thought that made her kiss him again.

Then she heard Caitlin rustling in her crib and Erin
drew away.

"I should go…" Her voice trailed off, breathless.

Dean just grinned. "Yeah. You should."

Then he grabbed the dustpan to empty it out.

She watched him go, bemused at how natural this
felt. Having Dean in her house as they worked together.

He shot a glance over his shoulder and his smile
leaped across the distance between them.

As she walked to the bedroom it was as if she could
feel his eyes on her. Hope grew and she allowed herself hesitant glimpses of a future.

And that's when she got the text message.

Chapter Fourteen

"So. That's finally done." Dean set the last nail on the baseboards, then set the hammer and nail set aside. He was sweating and his leg hurt, but the job he and Erin had been working on all week was finished.

Now, instead of dingy carpet, warm wood covered the floor, gleaming in the afternoon light.

"It looks great," Erin said, her hands on her hips as she surveyed the new flooring. "I can't thank you enough."

He heard her thanks but sensed a tension that had been around since he'd arrived this morning. In fact it had started yesterday afternoon. After he kissed her.

He'd gone over that moment again and again. She was so happy then and he'd felt a real connection between them.

But when she went to get Caitlin she'd stayed so long in the bedroom he thought she wasn't coming back and when she did, she seemed tense.

"You're welcome," he said, carefully stretching out his cramped leg. He knew he'd pushed it a bit hard today, but in the last couple of days his movements felt less restricted. A month ago he would have been in agony by now. It was good to know the therapy was helping. "Are you sure it's what you want? You seem, I don't know, disappointed," he hedged, wondering if she would say anything to explain her subdued mood.

"I'm not. Truly." And as if to underline her approval she rushed over and grabbed him in a tight hug.

He wasn't expecting it and he lost his balance and fell backward. Fortunately a wall was right behind him, but he twisted his bad knee, which sent a jolt of pain up his leg, clear into his skull.

He clenched his teeth as he rode out the pain. Erin grabbed him by his shirt, hauling on him.

"I'm sorry," she said. "I didn't think you would fall. I thought you were getting better."

Her words were well meant and to some extent she was right. He had been getting better. In fact, he had had gone riding with Vic last weekend. Sure, approaching the horse he had to fight down his fluttering nerves and dread, and yes, he had to take his time getting on, but once he was mounted, his fears stilled. And once they got going, riding up to check the cows to see if they needed to be moved had given him a glimpse of hope of a future on the ranch.

He glanced over at Erin, who was watching him with guarded sympathy in her expression. Though he knew she was concerned, it still annoyed him. He didn't want sympathy from her. He much preferred the admiration he'd just seen.

"I'm okay," he grunted even as the pain slowly subsided.

"I'm sorry," she said again, reaching out to him and he had to push aside his own wounded pride.

"It's okay. I'm still a little shaky on my feet," he said, trying to ease away her concern with a joke. "Still a cripple."

Her eyes narrowed and she dropped her hands on her hips in a defensive posture. "Don't talk about yourself like that," she said her voice tight. Hard. "I hate it when you do that."

Her eyes were snapping and her mouth was tight and he got a glimpse of an agitation simmering since yesterday. She was always so easygoing, but she'd been kind of edgy all day. When he'd asked her if anything was wrong she'd brushed him off.

He was about to ask her again but she turned away, gathering leftover pieces of baseboard and tossing them into the garbage box.

He collected his tools, the two of them working in a strained silence he didn't know how to break.

A few moments later the tools were back in his truck, the furniture was back in place and it was getting dark. Almost supper time.

Each day he'd worked here she had invited him for supper but today he had other plans.

"So, to celebrate finishing the flooring I thought we could go to the Grill and Chill," he said. "What do you think?" Though it wasn't the most private place, he hoped they could talk and he could find out what was bothering her.

Erin bit her lip as she looked away. "I…I don't think that will work."

"Oh. Sure. Okay." He felt dumb for assuming and as he saw her apologetic look he couldn't help a feeling of foreboding.

"I appreciate the invite," she said, "But I'm tired

and I thought I would just stay home. Make some sandwiches."

He was about to say that he didn't mind, but he got the sense that she wasn't inviting him to share said sandwiches. "Sure. That's fine," he said, wishing he sounded more casual than he felt.

She looked at him then, but her expression was unreadable. For a panicky instant he thought she was going to tell him it was over, but then she laid her hands on his shoulders and stepping into his automatic embrace, she pressed a kiss to his lips, then laid her head on his chest.

Puzzled at her varying emotions, he held her close, laying his head on hers.

"You mean a lot to me, you know," she said.

Her comment should have encouraged him, but the somber tone of her voice created a niggle of unease.

"And you to me," he said, holding her even closer, as if to stop whatever hovered behind her. A shadow. Something he couldn't put his finger on.

She was the first to pull away and he laid his finger under her chin, gently tilting her face up to his. "Is everything okay?"

She nodded, but her eyes skittered away from him and he knew she was hiding something. But he also guessed she wasn't going to tell him.

Then Caitlin started crying and Erin pulled away, hurrying to the bedroom. He heard the baby stop and then Erin's soothing voice as she changed her daughter.

Dean waited until she came back, still uncomfortable with how things were between them but not sure how or what he had to fix.

Erin came out of the bedroom holding Caitlin up

against her, the baby's head tucked into her neck. Dean felt his insides melt at the sight and he wanted to take Caitlin from Erin. Hold her himself.

He was surprised at how paternal he felt about the little girl. There was a little curl of panic inside him at the thought that things were off between him and Caitlin's mother.

"I'm going now," he said as Erin looked up at him. "Will I see you tomorrow? At church?"

"Of course." Her matter-of-fact tone reassured him.

"Good. Do you want me to pick you up?"

"Thanks, but I'd like to take my own car. Just in case Caitlin's not feeling well. But I'll be in church."

Again he felt brushed aside.

"Okay. Well, if I don't see you there, then I'll be back Monday to finish up the siding."

He took a chance and walked to her side, bending over to brush a gentle kiss on her cheek, then on Caitlin's head. "See you both tomorrow," he whispered, touching the baby's soft hair.

He caught Erin's expression then and saw a yearning in her eyes. But as he left he couldn't completely erase his concern.

Caitlin twisted and wriggled as Erin got to her feet to sing the opening songs of the church service. All the way to church this morning Caitlin had been squirming in her car seat as if she didn't want to go.

As if she sensed the stress her mom was dealing with.

"Do you want me to take her?" Dean asked as she tried to settle her daughter.

"It's okay. If she gets really bad I'll take her downstairs."

He held her eyes, his gaze questioning, but Erin looked away, trying to still her disquiet as she followed the singing. Sam's text on Friday afternoon had unnerved her. He was supposed to be out of her life. Supposed to be leaving her alone.

She hadn't responded, but he'd sent a few more on Saturday morning. Then he'd called. She hadn't answered and he'd left a message. She knew she should have ignored the voice mail, but she couldn't. His too-familiar voice told her that he wanted her back in his life and needed to talk to her.

When Dean came yesterday to finish the flooring, she hadn't been able to shed the clawing feelings of trepidation. Consequently she'd been out of sorts with Dean and she guessed he sensed it.

She shot him a quick sidelong glance and was rewarded with a wide smile and the light touch of his hand on her shoulder. But she could see the questions in his eyes. She knew he had picked up on her anxiety.

She forced her attention back to the song, trying to draw strength and encouragement from the words.

"Though the earth beneath me move, though the heavens move mightily, God who holds the stars will never abandon me."

Erin clung to the promise given to her not only in the song but also in the many Bible passages she'd been reading the past while. Though she had turned away from God, she knew He had always been there, waiting for her to come back. And now, as she stood beside Dean, she felt the assurance of that promise.

And yet Sam hovered in the background.

What did he want now? What did he hope would happen?

Caitlin tossed her head back again and let out a little cry. Erin knew she wouldn't be able to concentrate on the sermon if Caitlin got worse.

She tapped Dean on the shoulder to get his attention and he bent his head to catch her words.

"I'm going to bring her to the nursery," she said.

"You want me to come with you?" he asked, touching her shoulder in a gesture that was both assuring and comforting.

"I'll be okay."

She grabbed the diaper bag she had packed that morning and walked down the aisle, catching people's understanding smiles as she left.

Why had she thought she would be met with condemnation, she wondered as she walked down the steps? Since she had come back to Saddlebank as a single mother, the only time she'd felt uncomfortable was when Kelly had made her somewhat snide comment her first day here about how people could change. For the rest, everyone had been unfailingly understanding and caring.

And then there was Dean…

Again she felt a shiver of apprehension as thoughts of Sam shadowed thoughts of Dean. She and Dean were becoming closer and she had allowed herself hazy dreams of a future with him.

But as she walked down the stairs to the nursery, second thoughts dogged every step.

I need to tell him.

And hopefully when she did, Dean would understand.

She followed the signs to the nursery. As she came to the large counter between the hallway and the nursery, a woman with long dark hair and expressive amber eyes saw her and hurried over.

Abby Bannister. Erin remembered that she would be taking the photographs at Jodie and Finn's wedding and that she was married to their distant cousin, Lee Bannister.

"Hey, Erin, did you give up on keeping her in church?" she asked, grabbing a clipboard and a pen and setting them in front of Erin.

"She's been fussy. I can stay with her."

"No need for that. We'll take care of her." Abby grabbed a page of stickers and quickly wrote Caitlin's name on one without asking. Again Erin had that feeling of belonging.

"Any special instructions?" Abby asked as she pasted a sticker on the back of Caitlin's little dress.

"She's been fed and changed. There is a bottle in the bag if she needs it and a second set of clothes." Erin first handed her Caitlin, then the oversize bag that she had spent all morning packing up, unpacking and packing again. "I think everything is in there. If she cries, you'll call me, right?"

Abby's encouraging smile made her feel like she was being overly cautious. "Her number is 28. We'll flash it on the screen if she gets out of control."

Erin nodded, knowing this was for the best. Then, before she could change her mind, she hurried back the way she came. She wanted to be with Dean. To be standing beside him, worshipping. Being connected by their shared faith.

* * *

The last notes of the final song resounded through the sanctuary and Dean felt a sense of well-being wash over him. The sermon was encouraging and the songs uplifting.

But almost as important, Erin had sat beside him through the service, her hand twined in his.

It was as if the discomfort of yesterday was eased away in the space of the service. He thought she might be uncomfortable with Caitlin downstairs, but she didn't seem bothered by it.

And it was nice to spend time with her, even if it was in church, just the two of them.

He turned to Erin and was pleased to see her return his smile with a broad one of her own.

"I should get Caitlin," she said as people dispersed.

"Before you do, I'd like to ask you if you'd be willing to come to my mom's place for lunch."

She gave him a peculiar look. Had he pushed things too quickly? Though he'd had lunch last week with her aunt, it still seemed different for her to come to his mother's place. He felt as if it took their relationship to another level. Meeting parents made their situation more permanent and formal.

But then her bright smile melted away his misgivings. "I'd love to," she said, touching his arm with her hand.

He wanted to say more, but just then Keira and Tanner Fortier joined them. Tanner held a baby in the crook of one arm, looking as if he had done this all his life.

Keira caught Erin by the arm, grinning at her. "Hey, cousin, I haven't had a chance to see you since you came."

He saw Erin's face twist and she caught Keira in a hug. "It's been ages," she said, her voice muffled against Keira's neck. Then they pulled back, still holding onto each other's arms, their eyes looking each other over as if taking stock of the changes time had wrought.

Dean knew some of Keira's story. Knew that she and Tanner were once engaged. That Keira had mysteriously called it off and then disappeared for a while. She had come back to Saddlebank to take over her father's saddle-making business. When Tanner had come back to get his own saddle repaired they had gotten back together again. Now they were married.

Even though the circumstances were different, their story gave Dean hope for his own happy-ever-after with Erin.

They were chattering away, intently catching up so Dean tapped Erin lightly on the shoulder. "I'll get Caitlin," he said.

Erin glanced over and looked like she was about to protest.

"I won't drop her," he said with a half smile.

"I wasn't thinking that," she sputtered.

Then he gave her a grin to show her he was teasing. "Just stay. You two look like you need to catch up. I'll be right back."

To his surprise Erin nodded. So he left and while he made his careful way down the stairs he sent up a prayer that he wouldn't fall down. He waited in line to get Caitlin, exchanging smiles with the other mothers and feeling very much a sensitive and caring man. But when it finally came time for him he found out that Caitlin was gone. Jodie had already been there and had taken her. Stifling his annoyance at the missed chance to prove himself capable of helping Erin and capable of doing this small job, he turned to leave.

He slowly worked his way up the stairs, disappointed at the sudden twinge he felt. All part of the process, Mike had told him whenever Dean felt like he was going backward in his therapy.

But his limp was more noticeable as he got to the top of the stairs. He paused, hoping the unexpected pain would ease away. Then he saw Erin and his heart stilled.

She was talking to a man wearing a suit like it was a second skin, his hair cut like he had just stepped off the cover of *GQ*. He didn't look familiar. At all.

But from the way Erin was talking to him and the way he leaned toward her, his hand on her arm, he guessed she knew him well.

He limped over and as he joined them he caught the man's eye's shifting to him, then a frown creased his forehead.

Erin turned to him and he saw fear flicker in her eyes and then relief.

"Dean, I'm glad you're here." She sounded breathless. Had this man created that flush on her cheeks, the glisten in her eyes?

"I think Jodie picked up Caitlin—"

"I'd like you to meet Sam," she said cutting him off midsentence, gesturing toward the man standing so confidently in front of them.

Sam. The name rang like an alarm in his head.

Sam. The old boyfriend. The father of Erin's child.

"Actually, it's Dr. Sibley," Sam said with a condescending tone.

Which immediately set Dean's hackles up and made him suddenly aware of his own faded jeans, worn boots and shirt that should probably have been ironed before he put it on this morning.

Dean was no judge of clothes, but even he could see that this man's suit wasn't bought off the rack. That he didn't get his hair cut at the local barber.

Dean had never felt more like a hick than now.

"I noticed you were limping when you came here. You hurt yourself?" Sam—correction, Dr. Sibley—asked.

Dean wondered why he cared or why he thought it necessary to point out. "Rodeo injury."

Sam nodded slowly, then looked over at Erin, shifting his body, effectively turning his back to Dean.

"Do you have to be anywhere?" he asked her, putting his arm across Erin's shoulders in a proprietary gesture. "We have lots to talk about. Catch up on. I have important news for you."

Dean couldn't help a shiver of apprehension at the man's smug tone. The way he assumed that Erin would simply go along with him.

Erin shot a panicked look at Dean and he was about to intervene. To tell the guy to buzz off and leave them both alone.

But to his shock and dismay Erin turned back to Sam. "I can spare a little time for you."

"Excellent." Then without even a backward glance at Dean, his arm still draped over Erin's shoulders, Sam escorted her away.

Dismissed, Dean thought, hands curled into fists at his sides as he watched them leave, panic and fear coiling in his gut. He wanted to run after them, to ask

Erin what was going on. To ask why she was going with this guy.

Ice slipped through his veins.

Maybe Sam wanted Caitlin and Erin. Maybe, just maybe, he wanted them to be a family. Maybe he wanted to get together again.

He couldn't stay here and witness this.

He spun around and limped back through the sanctuary, heading toward another exit. He didn't want to see Erin with this man.

Caitlin's father.

A doctor. A successful man who had so much more to offer her than he did.

A messed-up, washed-up ex–rodeo cowboy.

Chapter Fifteen

"Why did you come here?" Erin demanded as soon as she and Sam were out of the building.

A chill autumn wind whistled around the church, making her shiver both with apprehension and from the cold.

Though she felt horrible about ditching Dean, she wanted to separate him and Sam as quickly as possible. She didn't want Dean to find out this way the truth about her relationship with her very ex boyfriend.

And she prayed, hard, that Jodie wouldn't come looking for her, carrying the baby Sam had told her to abort.

Sam reached out to touch her and she pulled herself back.

"I came looking for you, babe," he said, looking puzzled at her reaction.

"Why now?" She dared look at him and was pleased that those pale green eyes that could at one time send pleasant shivers down her spine no longer affected her.

"Look, I know I was wrong. I shouldn't have left you in the lurch like that. I got scared. But everything's changed now. I'm divorced. I left Helen. I knew it wasn't right to love you and stay married to her."

Each word falling from his full lips was like a blow.

"You're divorced?"

"Yes. Like I said, I love you. I did it for you."

He spoke the words like they were supposed to be a signal for her to fly into his arms. Instead they made her ill to think of his wife and child alone because of her.

When he reached for her again she pulled back. "Don't touch me," she said, her voice full of contempt and anger.

"But babe…"

"And stop calling me that. I'm not a horse."

"What?"

She waved off his puzzled question, her anger and frustration vying with a sick fear of what he had done because of her. "I don't want to have anything to do with you. I would never have gotten involved with you if I had known you were married."

"My marriage to Helen was a mistake."

"You had a child," she ground out, her hands now hard fists at her sides. "You had a child you were responsible for and who depended on you."

"When I met you, I knew how much I had been missing out on," he said, ignoring her accusations. "You were—are—so much more to me than Helen ever was. I've missed you so much. I haven't stopped thinking about you. So beautiful and precious."

Erin could only stare at him, trying to figure out what she ever saw in this man who seemed to think that now that he was supposedly free she would be more than willing to take him back.

She mentally compared him to Dean and in every respect this man fell short.

"Just go away. Stop phoning me and leave me alone." She wanted him gone before Jodie found her. Before Sam found out that she hadn't done as he asked and gotten rid of the baby she was carrying. Before he might decide to exercise his rights as a father. "You were a mistake I never should have made. I don't care for you one iota. You mean nothing to me. Less than nothing," she amended.

"You can't mean that." He took a step closer, reaching out to her again. "We were so good together."

She cringed at the memory and his words and stepped back. "I'm leaving now. Don't contact me ever again. We are done. Over."

And before he could say anything else, she strode back to the church, her heart beating a heavy rhythm, her blood surging. As the door to the outside thudded shut behind her, cutting her off from Sam, she stopped where she was, waiting to make sure he didn't follow her.

But the door didn't open and finally, a few minutes later, she dared to leave.

She went to find Dean and her daughter, hoping she'd find both at the same time.

Jodie stood at the back of the sanctuary, still holding Caitlin, chatting with Aunt Laura. Erin shot another glance behind, but Sam hadn't followed her.

"Have you seen Dean?" she asked as she gently extricated Caitlin from Jodie's arms.

"No. I thought he was with you." Jodie looked puzzled as she handed Erin her daughter's diaper bag.

"He was, but then…" Erin let the sentence fade away as she hooked the heavy bag over her shoulder.

"Goodness, girl, are you okay?" Aunt Laura asked. "You look pale as an Easter lily."

It was that obvious?

"I'm okay," Erin said, waving off her concern. "Just tired." The eternal excuse of any young mother.

"And who was that man you were talking to?" Aunt Laura asked. "He didn't look familiar."

"An acquaintance from back in California." Erin ignored Jodie's questioning look. "Someone I used to know." She looked around, hoping to catch a glimpse of Dean.

But she didn't see him. Which meant she would have to call to see if his invitation to have lunch at his mother's still stood. She knew she shouldn't have walked away from him, but she'd been afraid and had panicked. She didn't want him to find out from Sam that he had been married while they were dating.

You have to tell Dean. He needs to know the truth.

The pernicious voice just wouldn't leave her alone. She knew how he talked about Tiffany and how angry he'd been when he found out that she had dumped him for his brother. That she'd been pining for Vic even while she was dating Dean.

What would he think of her?

And would Sam stick around? He had come all this way; she doubted he would simply leave because she asked him to.

She pulled in a long, slow breath, trying to quiet the roiling questions.

"Can you come for lunch again?" Aunt Laura was asking.

Erin thought of Dean's invitation and shook her head. "Sorry, Aunt Laura, I'm not feeling well. I think I'll just go home." There was no way she could visit and make idle chitchat either with her aunt or Dean's mother. Not when she felt as if she were being sucked into a storm of events she couldn't stop.

Jodie shot her a questioning glance and Erin prayed that her sister would simply take her excuse at face value and not grill her. She couldn't handle any questions right now.

She needed to talk to Dean. Needed to connect with him and explain.

"Poor girl." Aunt Laura patted her shoulder gently, then stroked Caitlin's head. "You be good for your mommy now," she said, smiling down at her great-niece.

Caitlin's mouth twitched and then she seemed to break into a smile.

Erin's heart stuttered at the sight and behind her daughter's first true smile came the words of the song they'd been singing.

"Though the earth beneath me move, though the heavens move mightily, God who holds the stars will never abandon me."

She had to cling to that promise now. To trust that whatever happened, God would be with her and her little girl.

"Sorry, Mom, but there's been a change in plans." Dean grabbed a saddle one-handed from the shed, set it on his hip and walked over to his horse, Duke, while he held his cell phone with the other. A cool wind whistled through the trees edging the corral, scattering orange and gold leaves through the air. Winter was coming. "Erin had other things to do so I thought I would go riding instead."

"Can she come another time?"

Dean heard the disappointment in his mother's voice. She'd been thrilled when he asked if Erin and Caitlin could come for lunch and he knew, in her mind, she was already planning a wedding.

His mom tended to jump ahead like that.

"I don't know. We'll see." Too easily he remembered the sight of the very successful Dr. Sam Sibley. Handsome. Self-assured. Well-off. And the way he talked to Erin, it was as if he was once again laying his claim to her.

What chance did he have? So he left without checking to see if she was still coming, guessing that her plans had changed.

He tucked his phone under his ear as he hefted the saddle up and settled it on Duke.

"You didn't do anything, did you?"

"No, Mom. She just had something else going on." He wanted to sound reassuring, but he had a hard time believing this man wasn't insinuating himself back in Erin's life.

The biggest obstacle to his own plans for Erin was the fact that Dr. Sam was Caitlin's father. When he had asked Erin if Caitlin's father was involved she had been so adamant he wasn't. But what would she do now that he was back? Would she see the necessity of Caitlin having a father?

He remembered a conversation they'd had about her father. How she wanted so badly for any child of hers to have a secure, stable family.

And what could be more secure than to end up with the biological father of her daughter?

"So are you at the Rocking M?"

"No. Just on the yard here."

"Oh." In that single syllable he heard her question. Why didn't he come into the house?

Because he was a coward and didn't want to see first-hand his mother's disappointment. Though his invitation to Erin had simply been for lunch, he'd also never brought any other girl, not even Tiffany, to his home.

So they both knew what this simple visit represented.

"I just thought I would let you know I'm going riding up into the back pasture. Vic was going to check the cows to see if they needed to be moved so I thought I would do it for him."

"Should you do that alone? Shouldn't Vic be helping you? You haven't ridden for a while."

"I'll be fine, Mom." His comment came out more abruptly than he liked, but his frustration with Erin, Sam and his own situation leeched into his voice. He took a breath and then in a softer tone of voice said, "Truly, Mom, I'll be okay. But can you make sure Lucky doesn't follow me? I tied her up but she might pull loose."

"Yes. Of course. I can do that." Again he heard the edge of disappointment that he had tied up their dog but couldn't come into the house. He shrugged it off, ended his phone call with his mother and then turned the ringer off.

Erin had tried to call him a few times but he was afraid to answer. He didn't want to hear her carefully worded apology. Didn't want to hear her telling him that Caitlin's father was back in her life and that being with him was the right thing to do.

He simply didn't want to face the potential rejection. He'd thought losing Tiffany was difficult, but he had woven more fantasies around Erin and her baby than he ever had around Tiffany.

Erin had always been a part of his dreams. And now, even more than before.

With quick movements he got the saddle on Duke, tightening the cinch, then slipping on the bridle. He took a deep breath as he finished buckling the headstall. He looped the halter rope around the saddle, gathered the reins and then, quickly, before he chickened out, grabbed the saddle horn and shoved himself off.

To his relief and immense surprise, though he felt a twist of pain, it was nothing like it had been. And as he set his feet in the stirrups and pulled gently to one side on the reins and nudged Duke in the side, he felt a tiny victory.

One good thing Erin had brought to his life. It was because of his pride that he had gotten on a horse for the first time, and it was because he wanted to be better for her that he returned to therapy. Thanks to both those events, he sat on his own horse, riding out on his own for the first time since his accident.

And now, because of that same girl, his heart was shattered and broken.

Despair washed over him and he struggled to shake it off, clinging to the promises he'd heard in the sermon and in the songs they'd sung. That though people may let us down and life may bring its disappointments, God was faithful and that He held us close.

Dean had learned this lesson before, but it seemed to bear repeating.

Forgive me, Lord, for depending on things and people to bring me happiness, he prayed as he led his horse through the trees raining their leaves down on him. *Help me to put my trust in You. And only in You.*

And with that prayer echoing in his mind he straightened his shoulders and allowed himself to enjoy his small accomplishment.

As for Erin?

He knew he would have to find a way to release her. To do what he knew was best for her and for her baby.

Yet a part of him fought that. Was he really ready to just let her go?

He nudged his horse in the side, shifting it from a walk to a trot as if to outrun the question. But soon he felt the first jolt of pain shoot up his leg, so he pulled the horse back.

Baby steps, he reminded himself. But for now he was thankful he could get back on the horse on his own.

As for Erin, he needed to calm his own fears.

Maybe he should take a chance and talk to her face-to-face.

Tomorrow. When he went to work on the house. He would talk to her then.

For the fourth time that morning Erin picked up her phone to call Dean and then put it down again.

Yesterday after church, when she'd heard he was gone, she assumed his invitation to have lunch at his place had been withdrawn. She'd tried a couple of times to connect with him, but her calls had gone directly to voice mail. She hadn't left a message. What could she possibly say? How could she explain what had happened Sunday morning when Sam showed up?

Deep in her heart she'd hoped he would call her back, but that didn't happen, either. *He's coming to work on the house,* she told herself, looking away from her cell phone. *You can talk to him then. Face-to-face.*

She clicked her computer's mouse to open her latest project.

It was for an advertisement for a new line of paper her client was putting out. She'd just got the go-ahead email late Thursday night. A month ago she'd sent them a basic proposal knowing she was competing with dozens of other graphic artists. But thankfully, she'd been chosen and had been thrilled and grateful for the work. She was looking forward to sharing the news with Dean.

But then Sam had sent his first text.

He'd called a number of times this morning as well, but she'd simply let the phone go to voice mail.

The same thing, she suspected, Dean had done to her.

She forced herself to concentrate. She'd been roughing out some ideas for the papers, trying to create the sense of fun and excitement the company wanted. In the years she'd been doing this Erin had learned to look at ordinary objects from a different angle and connect with the ideas the customer hoped to present.

She'd come up with a basic concept. A stop-motion video of the various colors of the company's papers flipping like book pages and each one morphing into butterflies that would then fly up and...

This was where she got stuck. She had thought to

render the video so the butterflies would blend and spin to become the company logo, but the logo was bland and uninteresting. So she thought of getting them to change into a catchphrase that encapsulated what the company did.

But she hadn't figured that one out, either.

Usually it wasn't difficult to come up with concepts. But she couldn't concentrate today. The last time this happened was when she'd found out she was pregnant with Caitlin, but she had gotten through that.

However, this time she felt as if more was at stake. When she'd found out about Sam's deceit, anger had been her foremost emotion. Behind that had been shame at what she had participated in.

But now a deeper fear crept around the periphery of her thoughts. What if Dean didn't want her anymore?

Let go. You haven't talked to him yet. You can explain everything when he comes.

But the thought of having to tell him exactly what had happened between her and Sam and the fallout for his wife and child created a spiraling dread in the pit of her stomach.

Caitlin's sudden cries created a thankful distraction.

Her little girl lay in her crib, hands clenched in fists, her fitful cries tugging at Erin's heart. But as soon as she saw Erin, she stopped, her smile sudden and breathtaking.

"Oh, baby girl," Erin cooed, carefully picking her up and cradling her soft warmth in her arms so she could better see her face. "Was that a smile for Mommy? Did you have a smile for me?"

Caitlin's response was an even wider smile and a

wiggle of her little body as if she couldn't contain her own happiness.

Erin closed her eyes as she rocked her baby. "I love you so much," she whispered, her heart twisting at the thought of Sam somewhere in the vicinity. What would he say if he stayed and saw her? Would he want to be involved?

Erin pushed the thoughts aside and, as she had all night, sent up another prayer for patience and trust.

Our lives are in Your hands, Lord, she prayed. *Please take care of us.*

A knock on the door broke into the moment and she felt her soul lift. Dean was here.

She wanted to rush to the door, but the vain part of her stopped by her mirror to check the hair she had painstakingly brushed and braided this morning, smooth the yellow sweater she had chosen because Dean had, at one time, mentioned he liked yellow.

She drew in a shaky breath knowing this was the moment of truth.

Please, Lord, let him understand, she prayed as she shifted Caitlin in her arms, tugged on her frilly pink dress and dropped a kiss on her forehead. She set Caitlin in her bouncy chair, hoping she would stay quiet for a few more minutes.

Then she hurried to the door, nerves and fear and anticipation swirling around her.

She stopped at the door just as another knock came. She pulled in a steadying breath and yanked it open.

"Hey, babe, I was wondering if I had the wrong house."

Erin could only stare at Sam, standing on her doorstep, his one hand resting on the door frame, the other on his hip. His blue-and-white striped shirt and art-fully faded blue jeans made him look much more casual, but the leather loafers and the cologne he wore underlined his success.

"What are you doing here?"

"I found out where you lived. Thought I would talk to you in a more private place."

Erin's heart plunged as he moved closer, his grin making him look as if he had every right to be there.

"I told you to leave me alone," she said, her heart now racing with a combination of fear and nerves.

"I was hoping to talk to you." He lowered his voice, taking her hands in his. "Please. Let me explain."

He could do that so well, she thought, as his eyes softened and his smile tipped his perfectly shaped lips just so, his hands gently caressing hers.

But what would have at one time melted her resistance now just served to make her angry.

She jerked her hands free and took a step back just as he stepped inside the door and closed it behind him.

"I just need to talk to you," he said, touching her.

Fear sliced through her, but she pushed it aside. Sam would never do anything to her.

Then Caitlin squawked and Erin's heart tripled its pace. She hurried over to Caitlin's chair and carefully took her out.

Please, Lord, was all she could pray as she snuggled her close and turned to face an incredulous Sam.

"Is that ours? It that baby ours?" he asked, pointing to Caitlin, his eyes wide, his mouth slipping open in surprise.

Erin fought down her panic and slowly nodded. "She's my daughter."

"I'm the father." He spoke the words in a matter-of-fact tone as he shoved his hand through his perfectly styled hair, rearranging the immaculate waves she knew he had probably spent too much time on.

"Yes. You are."

Her prayers were fragments of fear and concern as she faced him down. His features registered surprise, then slowly shifted.

Into anger.

"I thought I told you to get rid of it."

It. The single word laced with contempt was like an abomination. As if this precious child was no more than an inconvenience. But at the same time his reaction created a glimmer of hope.

"I didn't. I could never do that." Erin looked down at Caitlin's sweet head and brushed a kiss over her hair, holding her even closer as if to protect her from the horrible words that Sam tossed around.

"Don't tell me you expect me to help you out with her."

"Have I asked at all?"

"No."

"Can I see her?"

Erin wanted to say no. To run away and hide her. Once he saw her face and saw how beautiful she was he would want to be involved with her.

But he was her father and so she stifled her trepidation and gently turned her baby to see her father for the first time. Erin kept her eyes on Caitlin, not sure she wanted to see Sam's reaction.

"Oh, babe," he whispered, his voice holding a melancholy edge that frightened her.

He took a step closer, his hand reaching out. Erin's

heart thudded harder but all Sam did was lay his hand on Erin's shoulder and squeeze. "Why did you do this?" he asked.

"It was my choice." She looked up at him, fear lancing her at the anger in his expression. "I wanted her. I couldn't do what you asked."

"This wasn't supposed to happen. I told you to get rid of her." He squeezed harder. "I divorced Helen and walked away from her kid so I could be with you. I don't want any kids in my life to complicate things."

Suddenly fearful now, she pulled away from his grasp and he released her, his hand dropping to his side.

"So you don't want any part of Caitlin?" she asked.

He shook his head, his hand slicing the air between them. "I never wanted kids. That's why I fought with Helen. I thought you…you would understand."

She wasn't sure why he assumed that, but she didn't want to get into that discussion now.

"So you aren't going to claim any rights to Caitlin?"

"No. Never. I don't want to have anything to do with her." His expression grew pleading. "I just wanted you to be with me. No one else getting in the way."

She could only stare at him, wondering how he thought she would have ever agreed to this. But even more importantly, wondering what she had ever seen in this self-centered, venal man. The thought made her almost as sick as the words Sam had been saying to her.

"So you just walked away from your other responsibilities thinking I would gladly take up with you?" She couldn't begin to articulate the disgust she felt for him.

"Yeah. I guess so."

"I would never do that. Even if I didn't have Caitlin. Once I found out you were married, it was over between us."

"I told you, I never loved Helen." His anger had shifted and now he was almost begging. "I only loved you. I want us to be together. But now... Now you've got this baby. That changes everything."

"Enough," she snapped, taking control of the situation, her voice growing hard. "You didn't want me to keep Caitlin and you don't want to take responsibility for her, is that right?"

"Yes. Of course it is."

Erin's shoulders sagged with relief but she knew she wasn't done yet. "I want that in writing. In front of a lawyer."

Sam just stared at her, as if he couldn't understand this person she'd become.

Then his features hardened. "Works for me. I don't want any part of any kid." He almost snorted. "And I want to make sure you won't come after me for child support."

"I wouldn't take one penny from you," she said.

Sam looked around her house, his eyes narrowing. "Well, if this is the kind of life you want for your daughter..." He turned back to her, not finishing the sentence, his tone saying everything his words didn't. "And I suppose you're dating that cripple—"

"Don't you even mention him." Her eyes narrowed, her teeth clenched in rage as she resisted the impulse to slap his face. "Dean is ten times, no, one hundred times the man you are."

Erin grabbed Caitlin's diaper bag, the jacket she had draped over the back of her chair and tucked both over her arm. "Let's go to town," she said. "The sooner we get this done, the happier I'll be."

Sam hesitated and for a heartrending moment she thought he was changing his mind.

"We would have been so good together, babe," he whispered.

"No. We wouldn't have. The only good thing that came out of being with you was my daughter. Now let's finish this."

Chapter Sixteen

Dean turned his truck around and drove down the highway toward home, his hands wrapped around his steering wheel.

Erin had called him numerous times, but she hadn't left a message. He wished he could simply let it go, but he was concerned.

But then he'd arrived at her place in time to see Sam get out of his fancy red sports car and step into Erin's house.

Dean gritted his teeth, fighting down his own fears. This was only right. Erin had grown up in a fractured family. Getting back together with Sam, the father of her child, was the right thing.

So why did it make him feel so hollow inside?

Why did he constantly compare himself to the suave, rich-looking guy who looked as if he could give Erin anything she ever wanted or needed?

He drew in a deep, slow breath and struggled, once again, to give his life over to God. To let go of control. It had been hard enough when he was laid up in the hospital facing an uncertain future.

But now, even though his leg was better, his future as far as work was concerned was brighter, what he wanted more than anything was out of his reach.

Vic was in the corrals when he got back home, reinforcing fences and getting them ready for when they brought the cows back down from pasture and they would process them.

He lowered his hammer when he saw Dean walking toward him.

"What's up? Aren't you supposed to be working at Erin's place?"

Dean walked through the gate and picked up the fence tightener. "I'm not working there anymore."

Vic frowned as he finagled another staple out of the pail in front of him. "Why not?"

Dean tightened up the wire as Vic pounded the staple in. "Don't feel like being there. Jan can send someone else to finish up."

Vic rested his hammer on the fence post, turning to his brother. "What's going on?"

Dean moved a little further down the fence line and reattached the tightener. Vic stayed where he was, waiting. Dean suspected he wasn't going to leave him alone until he spilled.

"Erin's old boyfriend came back. Caitlin's father."

"When?"

"Yesterday. At church. They were talking privately."

"So that's why Erin and Caitlin didn't come here for lunch?"

"I figured she'd want to spend time with him." Dean didn't want to admit that seeing Sam all dressed up and looking so successful had sent him scurrying away before he knew exactly what was going on.

"He's there right now," Dean added. "I saw him go into her house."

"So they're getting back together?"

"He's Caitlin's father. So I'm guessing she would want to do the right thing. I mean, she grew up without her dad around a lot. Divorced parents. I know she wants only what's best for Caitlin."

"Did she tell you she was seeing him again?"

"Well, why wouldn't she?"

"So you didn't actually talk to her?"

Dean yanked on the tightener. He should have just gone straight to the house. He didn't need this, though that meant dealing with questions from his mother. He wasn't sure which was worse.

"What's to talk about?" Dean returned finally. "He's Caitlin's father. He can provide a life for her and Erin that I couldn't begin to."

"How do you figure that?"

"He's a doctor, Vic. He drives a car that's worth ten times what my truck is. He's not some…crippled cowboy." Dean didn't want to look up at his brother. Didn't want to see the pity in his expression, but it was as if he couldn't stop himself. And when he snagged his brother's gaze he saw not pity, but exasperation.

"Why do you talk about yourself like that?" Vic ground out, his one hand clenched around the hammer. "Like you're looking for sympathy."

"I'm not—"

"Ever since your accident you've been putting yourself down. Seeing yourself as less than who you really are. Why do you do that? Why are you putting down what God has done in you?"

Dean was shocked at his brother's anger, but Vic's words also created an answering shame.

"It's not that," he protested. "It's just for Erin's sake. I can't do for her what that other guy can."

"If that other guy was so great, don't you think she would have stayed with him?" Vic crossed his arms over his chest, his expression softening. "Don't minimize what you have to give to someone like Erin. You're a great guy. You'd make an amazing father. And I'm sure she cares a lot for you. At least that's what I've been hearing through Lauren. And if anyone should know, her twin sister should."

Dean let his brother's words assure him but at the same time he couldn't rid himself of a niggling feeling that Erin would want to do the right thing. And as far as he could see, that would be staying with Caitlin's father.

"You don't look convinced," Vic said.

Dean sighed, leaning on the fence post, looking out over the yard. The place that had been his home all these years. A place he had never wanted to leave and a place that, for a time, he thought he would settle down with Erin and Caitlin as a family.

"Erin grew up with a part-time father. I know she wants more than that for her daughter. If there's a chance—"

"You don't think you can be that father?" Vic interrupted him.

"I haven't lived the best life. I haven't been the best person. Erin turned me down all those years ago for a good reason. And now, compared to this guy—"

"Stop it. Stop comparing yourself." Vic walked over to Dean and put his hands on his shoulders and gave him a light shake. "You may not have been the best per-

son at one time in your life, but who of us have? We all
have made mistakes. Done things we have had to ask
God's forgiveness for. But you never hurt anyone. You
never caused anyone sorrow or grief. The mistakes you
made were your own. And the one thing you have truly
going for you is your faithful love for that girl. Even
when you were dating Tiffany I know you mentally
compared her to Erin. In many ways, you've probably
been the most faithful person in her life."

Dean felt a warm glow at his brother's words. At the
comfort he knew Vic was trying to give him.

"I know she cares about you, Dean," Vic continued. "You shouldn't assume that just because this guy
is back she wants him in her life. You should probably
find this out for yourself."

Dean nodded slowly, recognizing the wisdom in
what his brother was saying.

He knew it would be hard. It would mean putting
himself at risk of being rejected by Erin McCauley
yet again.

Could he do it?

"Let's finish this fence" was all he said to Vic. But
as they worked in silence, the thin warmth of the sun
slowly waning, Dean couldn't let go of what Vic had
told him.

Later that night, alone in his bedroom, the one he'd
stayed in since he was a young boy, he took his Bible
and flipped through it, looking for the passages that
had given him comfort when he was in the hospital,
thinking his life was over.

He had made a choice then to let go of himself. To
let go of what he thought his life should look like. It

hadn't been easy, but he'd been comforted by the passage in front of him.

In repentance and rest is your salvation. In quietness and trust is your strength.

He had always found it interesting that in the middle of woes and prophecies, in the middle of seeming chaos were these two lines that promised so much more.

It was like his own life. The mess, the busyness, the chasing after things that didn't satisfy.

In the middle of all of that had come these words to calm and still him and turn him in the right direction.

And now, as he felt as if his life was turned upside down yet again, he took these verses to heart.

In quietness and trust was his strength.

He had to let go of his pride and tell Erin what he needed to tell her. Not for his sake, but for hers. To give her a choice.

He bowed his head and slowly let God's peace wash over him. No matter what happened, he knew where his strength and peace lay.

Erin lay in bed, the morning light washing over her. She could only stare at the ceiling trying to absorb what had happened the last couple of days. On Sunday, Sam had showed up full of ridiculous hope that they could get back together again.

Then yesterday they had gone to the lawyer. She was happy that Drake Neubauer could take them in right away and was only too willing to help her draft an agreement. They got it notarized and it was over.

That shadow was removed from her life.

Sam had wanted to give her money, but she refused. She didn't want any connection to him in any way. The only thing she had wanted from him, he had given her reluctantly.

Helen's phone number.

He had looked regretful when he left and had tried to kiss her goodbye, but Erin had turned away. It was over.

She sat up slowly feeling a sense of emptiness in spite of the relief she felt at knowing that Sam was out of her and Caitlin's life. Dean hadn't come yesterday at all. Nor had he returned her calls from Sunday.

She wanted to call him again, but every time she picked up her phone guilt held her back. She knew she had to tell him everything about her relationship with Sam and should have a while ago.

Erin pushed herself out of bed and quickly got dressed. She would shower later. Once Caitlin was bathed and taken care of.

"Hey, baby girl," Erin whispered as she picked up her precious daughter. "It's a new day."

Caitlin cooed softly, then broke into a smile that dove straight into Erin's heart.

As she fed the baby she choked down a light sob at the emptiness that yawned ahead of her.

Why didn't Dean call her?

She shook off the questions and focused on feeding and bathing her daughter. Then dressing her in one of the many outfits her sisters and Aunt Laura kept buying for her. When she was finally done, she put Caitlin in her bouncy chair and sat down with her phone. One big thing needed to be done yet.

She swallowed as she pulled out the piece of paper Sam had given her and stared at the phone number she insisted he write on it.

Help me, Lord.

Then she dialed the number.

Helen answered on the first ring. As if she was anticipating her call.

"Hello, Erin" was her quiet response. She knew who was calling.

Erin swallowed at the reality that Helen could identify her number. Had she seen it on Sam's phone when they were seeing each other?

She fought down the shame once again and pressed on.

"I felt like I needed to call you," Erin said, glancing over at Caitlin, who was clean and fed and now so happy. How could such an adorable child have come from such perfidy?

She shook that thought off. She couldn't think of Caitlin that way. Her baby was a gift from God pure and simple.

"I'm glad you called," Helen said.

Erin felt confused. She hunched over, clinging to the phone, bewildered by Helen's response.

"Why are you glad? I would think you should be angry with me."

"I was. For a while. But you need to know that I forgive you. I know the breakup of our marriage wasn't your fault."

Erin sagged back against the couch, shocked at how easily Helen spoke those words.

"I don't feel like I deserve your forgiveness," she said, her voice quiet with shame.

"You do and you need to know that I should ask your forgiveness, as well. When I came to your place I was afraid. Clinging by the thinnest thread to a marriage that I should have known was over long before you came on the scene."

"What are you saying?"

"You weren't the first one Sam was cheating on me with. I found out that even while he was supposedly with you, he was seeing someone else, as well."

Shame engulfed her but behind that rose an anger with the man who had so brazenly shown up on her doorstep claiming that he loved her. What hubris. What arrogance.

"I'm so sorry" was all Erin could manage.

"Don't worry. You didn't break up our marriage. Sam did. I finally saw the light and divorced his sorry self."

"But he came here to tell me—"

"That he divorced me." Helen released a heavy sigh. "He's such a prideful idiot. I only wished I'd seen it sooner."

Erin was quiet as she grappled with what had just happened. The gentle promise of peace that lingered on the horizon. "Again. I'm sorry. Will you be okay?"

"I hit him financially for all I could," Helen said. "Every month when those withdrawals come out of his bank account he'll remember me. I'll be fine."

Erin didn't know what to say after that.

"Well, I don't suppose we'll be exchanging Christmas cards even though we have quite a bit in common," Helen said. "You take care of yourself. Please don't let what he did to you determine your self-worth. I know I had to struggle with it. I'm just glad I took control of my life. I hope you can do the same."

Erin let her comment settle in her soul. Helen seemed to know exactly what she was feeling.

Then as they said goodbye, she realized that Helen probably, better than anyone, knew what she was dealing with. The shame. The sense of being less than.

She looked around the house that she and Dean had spent time fixing up. The dreams she had woven around this home. Thinking that it would be a home for her and Dean and Caitlin.

She thought of what Helen had said. That she was glad she took control of her life.

Well, maybe it was time she did the same. Maybe it was time she faced down her fears. Realized she had much to give Dean. That Helen had forgiven her. That God had forgiven her. That in God's eyes she was valuable and important.

She needed to talk to Dean. To tell him the truth. To realize that she had made an innocent mistake.

Knowing that Helen had forgiven her made it easier to think that Dean might understand.

She packed up Caitlin's diaper bag and just as she grabbed her car keys off the key ring she heard a knock on the door.

Her heart jumped.

Was Sam back after all?

She hesitated, breathed a quick prayer, then slowly opened the door.

Dean stood there. Hat in hand.

But he wasn't smiling. "Can I come in?"

Erin simply nodded, then stood aside.

Dean looked around the house feeling a sense of pride in how good it looked.

He had been a part of this.

And, Lord willing, he still would.

He laid his hat on the table and turned to Erin, who was looking at him, apprehension in her eyes.

He wasn't sure what she was about to tell him. He didn't want to wait until she said that she and Sam were getting together. He needed to get this off his chest before he changed his mind.

He needed her to know that she had options. If he could be considered one.

"I need to tell you—"

"I have something you need to know—"

They both spoke at the same time and at her words Dean's heart sunk. But he shook his head, swallowed his pride and held up his hand.

"I'm going to be rude and ask if I can go first," he said. He drew in a shaky breath and forced himself to look deep into her eyes. "I don't know what's happening in your life right now. I don't know where you're at. But I need to tell you where I am." He paused as memories of Erin's previous rejections skimmed too easily back into his mind.

But he clung to the more recent memories. The kisses they'd shared. The work they had done together. He had to tell himself that what they'd had was real no matter what may happen in Erin's life. And that he too had something to offer her, as Vic had said.

"I want you to know that no matter what happens to you or has happened to you, I have always cared for you," he told her, his heart pounding in his chest now, knowing what was at stake. "You've always been a part of my life. You've always been the one I've used as my standard for any woman I've ever dated. They all fell short."

Her cry of dismay nearly stopped him.

"I love you," he said, pushing on before nerves and fear kept him from what he wanted to say. "I love your daughter. I know that Caitlin's father is back in her life and while I don't know what that means for you, I need you to know that I am willing to go with whatever happens because I only want what's best for you and for Caitlin. I know that you've lived without your father for many years and I know what it means for you to have an intact family. But I want you to know that I love you. I can't let you go without you knowing that."

She wasn't looking at him, but he could see tears running down her cheek. He wanted to grab her, pull her close, but he waited.

"Please say something," he finally asked, tossing his pride away yet one more time. "Tell me to leave. Ask me stay. Something."

"I want you to stay," she whispered.

As her quiet words registered his heart sang. But her tears confused him.

"Why are you so sad?" he said, laying his hands on her shoulders, trying to find his way through this situation. "Is it Sam?"

She shook her head, hard. "No. It's not Sam. He's gone. He's out of my life and Caitlin's."

Was that why she was crying?

"I'm so sorry to hear that," Dean said.

"It's not what you think." Finally she looked up at him, her eyes red-rimmed and brimming with tears. She put her hand on his chest, creating a small connection. "I sent him away. He didn't want to have anything to do with Caitlin and I didn't want to have anything to do with him. He hasn't meant anything to me since

I walked away from him after I found out I was pregnant."

Each word she spoke created another surge of hope. He gently brushed a tear from her face, still puzzled. "Then why are you crying?"

She swallowed, holding his gaze, her expression almost pleading. "Because you talk about me like I'm some wonderful person and I'm not."

"Erin, honey, you made a mistake. We all do. It doesn't mean you're a bad person—"

"He was married when I was dating him," Erin said suddenly. "He was committed to someone else."

Dean could only stare, trying to absorb what she was saying.

"He was married."

"Yes."

"Did he tell you?"

"Of course not."

"Then it was hardly your fault."

Erin held his gaze, her features softening. "So that doesn't matter to you?"

"What matters to me is that you're so upset."

Erin pressed her trembling lips together, looking away. "I thought you would be angry. I was so ashamed. Bad enough that I'd been intimate with a man as a single girl, worse that he was married. You always talk about me like I am such a good person, when I did this horrible thing."

"But you said you didn't know so it's not like you did this deliberately. It's his fault for being such a jerk."

She was silent a moment and Dean couldn't hold himself back. He pulled her into his arms, holding her close. "You are an amazing and wonderful and good person," he said, pressing a kiss to her forehead, then curling her head against him. "You really are. Nothing you tell me changes that. I've told you before that you were always an example to me of goodness and kindness and you still are."

Erin drew back, looking up at him, her face still holding shadows of sorrow. But in her eyes he saw a glimmer of hope.

"I love you," he said. "I think I always have."

Her smile brightened her face. "I love you, too. So much."

"I want to be a father to your little girl," he said. "To Caitlin. I want to be in your life."

And then he sealed that promise with a kiss.

Epilogue

The mini lights sparkled in the rafters of Finn's barn. Clusters of Christmas trees full of white lights and red balls were scattered along the hall. The tables covered with thick, white tablecloths held crystal vases filled with red balls. Red napkins tucked under plates carried out the color scheme Jodie had decided on as soon as she and Finn had settled on a winter wedding.

All the plans had come together for a fairy-tale wedding for Finn and Jodie.

Erin looked around the hall, but Dean was still gone.

The past few weeks were a whirlwind of preparations and decorating and last-minute running around. Also, between his therapy and helping Vic get the corrals ready on the Rocking M and her increasing work load, she and Dean hadn't spent much time together.

She had been looking forward to today, but they had only managed to spend some time together between the ceremony and picture taking. The men had been gone the past twenty minutes while Abby Bannister, the photographer, took a number of photos of just the sisters.

"Okay, girls," she was saying now. "One last one of the three of you by the largest Christmas tree."

"Can we just be done?" Jodie groaned as she gathered up the yards of raw silk that made up her wedding dress. "My feet hurt and I heard Santa Claus is coming for a visit."

Christmas wasn't for a couple of weeks yet, but that hadn't stopped Jodie from going all-out with a Christmas-themed wedding.

Or from getting someone to play Santa Claus for the kids that were in attendance.

Lauren just tut-tutted as she arranged one of Jodie's curls, then turned to Erin to help her, as well.

"I'm fine," Erin said, holding up her hand to forestall her sister's attempts at taming her hair. Caitlin had gotten her sticky fingers entangled in the curls Brooke had sprayed to battle-ready stiffness, and they were askew, but she didn't care. "And I'm with Jodie. I'm tired."

She was impatient to get the pictures done, as well. She wanted to find Dean.

But Lauren ignored her and pinned one of her curls back, smoothed out her dress and gave a decisive nod. "You look beautiful. And just relax. You only have to do this one more time. For my wedding."

Erin forced a smile. The thought of doing this all over again wasn't appealing.

"And don't look like I just asked you to help butcher chickens," Lauren admonished her. "You'll be glad to help out again. Just as I will be glad to help out when your time comes."

Her sister's comment was encouraging, but while she and Dean had been dating for a couple of months now he hadn't said much about their future and she wasn't about to bring it up. She was still learning lessons in trust, she realized.

The three girls obediently posed in front of the tree, gathering close, cheek to cheek, bouquets of red roses and white lilies close to their faces as cameras flashed all around them.

Finally Abby was finished, and Jodie and Erin both heaved a sigh of relief.

Erin hurried over to Heather, who was playing with Caitlin and her stepdaughter Adana, her stomach just starting to protrude. It was baby central in Saddlebank these days.

"So, she's adorable," Heather said, smiling up at Erin.

In spite of being dressed up and made up and hair professionally done, Erin felt just a bit dowdy around Heather. The former model was stunning, even pregnant and with a three-year-old toddler leaning against her, holding up a stuffed rabbit for Caitlin, who wasn't paying her any attention.

"I'm glad she's been good."

"She's been a perfect baby. I can only hope mine is as well behaved," Heather said.

"That would depend who she takes after. You or John," Abby joked as she joined them, then crouched down to snap a picture of Caitlin, who was grabbing at her satin shoes, gurgling and drooling all over the red silk dress Jodie had insisted on buying for her.

Erin looked around with a tiny niggle of anxiety. She saw Lee standing by Vic, Finn was now with Jodie, but she couldn't see Dean anywhere.

Then the jingle of bells sounded and Adana's head popped up as she heard a distinctive "Ho, Ho, Ho."

"Ith it Thanta Cwauth?" she lisped, eyes wide, staring past Erin to the entrance to the hall.

Erin and everyone else in the hall turned around in time to see a man dressed up in a Santa Claus suit complete with fake beard, fake belly, and the faintest limp enter the room.

"Merry Christmas," he bellowed, jingling the string of sleigh bells and looking around the room.

Erin just laughed.

Dean. Of course. No wonder he'd been so secretive.

He had a bag in his hand and he made his way to a large chair set aside and decorated for the occasion. The children in attendance crowded around him as he slowly sat down.

"One at a time," he bellowed in true Santa fashion. "One at a time."

Erin just smiled as she watched him with the children, her heart full of warmth and love for this man. He was such a natural. He took the time to talk to each child. To lean close and listen. He had a gift for each one as well and remembered who was who. No small feat considering there were about a dozen youngsters in attendance.

"I hear there's a baby here that needs a present yet," he called out when all the children were finished with him. "Caitlin. You tell your mommy to come and bring you here, too."

Chuckling, Erin took Caitlin from Heather and made her way through the excited children tossing wrapping paper aside as they tore into their gifts.

Out of the corner of her eye she saw Abby approach and her heart sank. More pictures?

She pushed the thought aside as she brought Caitlin to Dean.

He pulled them both onto his knee, his eyes twinkling underneath the fake eyebrows.

"So, have you been a good girl this year?" he asked.

"I tried," she returned.

"And how about this little one," he said, tickling Caitlin under the chin with his forefinger. "I'm sure she's been good," he said with forced heartiness.

"As good as gold."

"Of course she would be with such an amazing mother." Dean shifted his arm, reaching for his bag one-handed.

"So, why don't you tell me what you want for Christmas?"

He had dropped the fake Santa voice, speaking to her normally.

She looked deep into his eyes and said, "All I want for Christmas is you."

"Well, now, I think I can manage that," he said, his eyes twinkling. "But how about I tell you what I want for Christmas?"

"I didn't think Santa Claus had any wishes."

"Well, there's world peace and high cattle prices. And then there's this."

He dug into his bag and pulled out a tiny box.

Erin's heart stuttered in her chest. She hardly dared to believe what might be happening.

Dean flipped the box open and under the glow of Christmas lights the diamond on the band sparkled with hundreds of lights sending out rays of hope.

"Erin McCauley, will you marry me?"

His words resonated in the silence that had fallen on the gathering.

Erin's throat thickened with a myriad of emotions as she looked at the promise held in Dean's hand and echoed in his eyes.

All she could do was nod her agreement.

A huge cheer went up from the people now gathered around them as Dean slipped the ring, one-handed, onto her finger. Lights flashed as people took pictures. Erin ignored them all, pulled the fake beard down and kissed Dean fully on his lips.

He held her close, returning her kiss. Then he drew back, looking from her to Caitlin nestled between them.

"You know I love you dearly," he said. "I love you both. And I'll spend the rest of my life proving it."

"You don't have to prove anything," she said, as he stood up and pull her along.

He kissed her again and another cheer went up.

"Hey, Santa, what are you doing for an encore?" Vic asked, standing beside him, his arm draped over Lauren's shoulder.

"If I'd known he was giving out engagement rings, I might have stood in line myself," Jodie joked.

"You already have one," Finn growled. "And a wedding ring as well, I might add."

Jodie grinned up at him. "Just teasing."

Erin looked from Jodie and Finn to Lauren and Vic and all the people gathered around them, an accepting loving community who had taken her and Caitlin in. Her heart overflowed with happiness and joy and an incredible thankfulness.

"I think it will be a wonderful Christmas," Lauren

said, with a kiss to her sister, then her niece and finally giving Dean a hug.

"It's going to be amazing," Jodie said, laying her hand on Erin's shoulder. "And in the classic words of Tiny Tim, God bless us, every one."

Erin turned to Dean again. "I love you so much," she whispered.

"I love you, too."

She laid her head on his shoulder, and Dean curled his other arm around Caitlin, closing the circle and completing it.

A promise of the future. A family for both of them. A gift from God.

* * * * *

If you loved this story,
pick up the other BIG SKY COWBOYS *books,*
WRANGLING THE COWBOY'S HEART
TRUSTING THE COWBOY
and these other stories of love in Montana
from bestselling author Carolyne Aarsen
HER COWBOY HERO
REUNITED WITH THE COWBOY
THE COWBOY'S HOMECOMING

Available now from Love Inspired!
Find more great reads at www.LoveInspired.com

Dear Reader,

Pride is part of what this story is about. Dean's pride in his rough-and-ready self-suffiency and, to some degree, Erin's pride in her status as the "good girl." Both Erin and Dean's life were spun in circles by what happened to them and both had to learn to pick themselves up and accept themselves for who they were. To realize that God's acceptance mattered more than people's.

I think each of us has, inside of us, a better person they want to be. I know I do. But I fall short time and time again.

I'm so thankful that my salvation and strength do not depend on me. That repentance must be my daily attitude. Repentance and rest. I can trust that God forgives all the mistakes I make. The times I fall short. I am so thankful for the peace that gives me and I pray for the same peace for you.

Carolyne Aarsen

PS: Want to find out more about my other books? Check out my website at www.carolyneaarsen.com and reccive a free ebook for signing up for my newsletter. As well, I love to hear from my readers. You can write me at caarsen@xplornet.com.

REQUEST YOUR FREE BOOKS!

2 FREE INSPIRATIONAL NOVELS
PLUS 2
FREE
MYSTERY GIFTS

Love Inspired®

SPECIAL EXCERPT FROM

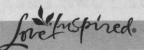

*Could a Christmastime nanny position for the ranch
foreman's son turn into a full-time new family for one
Texas teacher?*

Read on for a sneak preview of the third book in the
LONE STAR COWBOY LEAGUE: BOYS RANCH
miniseries, THE NANNY'S TEXAS CHRISTMAS
by Lee Tobin McClain.

"Am I in trouble?" Logan asked, sniffling.

How did you discipline a kid when his whole life had
just flashed before your eyes? Flint schooled his features
into firmness. "One thing's for sure, tractors are going to
be off-limits for a long time."

Logan just buried his head in Flint's shoulder.

As they all started walking again, Flint felt that delicate
hand on his arm once more.

"You doing okay?" Lana Alvarez asked.

He shook his head. "I just got a few more gray hairs. I
should've been watching him better."

"Maybe so," Marnie said. "But you can't, not with all
the work you have at the ranch. So I think we can all
agree—you need a babysitter for Logan." She stepped in
front of Lana and Flint, causing them both to stop. "And
the right person to do it is here. Miss Lana Alvarez."

"Oh, Flint doesn't want—"

"You've got time after school. And a Christmas
vacation coming up." Marnie crossed her arms, looking

determined. "Logan already loves you. You could help to keep him safe and happy."

Flint's desire to keep Lana at a distance tried to raise its head, but his worry about his son, his gratitude about Logan's safety, and the sheer terror he'd just been through, put his own concerns into perspective.

Logan took priority. And if Lana would agree to be Logan's nanny on a temporary basis, that would be best for Logan.

And Flint would tolerate her nearness. Somehow.

"Can she, Daddy?" Logan asked, his face eager.

He turned to Lana, who looked like she was facing a firing squad. "Can you?" he asked her.

"Please, Miss Alvarez?" Logan chimed in.

Lana drew in a breath and studied them both, and Flint could almost see the wheels turning in her brain.

He could see mixed feelings on her face, too. Fondness for Logan. Mistrust of Flint himself.

Maybe a little bit of… What was that hint of pain that wrinkled her forehead and darkened her eyes?

Flint felt like he was holding his breath.

Finally, Lana gave a definitive nod. "All right," she said. "We can try it. But I'm going to have some very definite rules for you, young man." She looked at Logan with mock sternness.

As they started walking toward the house again, Lana gave Flint a cool stare that made him think she might have some definite rules for him, too.

Don't miss
THE NANNY'S TEXAS CHRISTMAS
by Lee Tobin McClain, available December 2016
wherever Love Inspired® books and ebooks are sold.

www.LoveInspired.com

LIEXP1116

Turn your love of reading into rewards you'll love with
Harlequin My Rewards

**Join for FREE today at
www.HarlequinMyRewards.com**

Earn **FREE BOOKS** of your choice.

Experience **EXCLUSIVE OFFERS** and contests.

Enjoy **BOOK RECOMMENDATIONS**
selected just for you.

PLUS! Sign up now
and get **500** points
right away!

Earn
FREE
REWARDS
Join
Today!
HarlequinMyRewards.com

MYR16R